# KILL MCCORMICK

## BY STEVEN SHANNON

This novel in its entirety is a work of fiction. All the charters and incidents portrayed in this work are the result of author's imagination. Any resemblance to actual events or individuals, both living and dead, is entirely coincidental.

Copyright © Steven Shannon 2020

Steven Shannon asserts the moral right to be identified as the author of this work

Published by the Author

All rights reserved. No part of this publication may be reproduced, distributed, or transmitted in any form or by any means, including photocopying, recording, or other electronic or mechanical methods, without the prior written permission of the publisher, except in the case of brief quotations embodied in critical reviews and certain other non-commercial uses permitted by copyright law. For permission requests, write to the publisher, addressed "Attention: Permissions Coordinator".

## ABOUT THE AUTHOR

Steven Shannon

Steven Shannon is a pseudenom for the author of this book who was born in Ballymoney, Co Antrim in 1968. Two years later the "Troubles" in Northern Ireland began in earnest so the author knew nothing of 'normal' life until the 1994 ceasefire.

The Steven Shannon trilogy is fictional but based on a lifetime of the author watching the "Troubles" rage around him and drawing him into the heart of them.Shannon seeks to clarify the roles played by the various bodies involved in the conflict including the police, military intelligence , Loyalist and Republican paramilitaries as well as the ordinary people who sought to live normal lives in an abnormal society.

Vicious Circle

The first book in the three book series, Vicious Circle, tells the story of four young Loyalists motivated by revenge and frustration after the murder of their childhood friend, who go to war against Republicans. They are hotly pursued by a dogged police officer, Jim McCormick, and manipulated by shadowy figures from Military Intelligence.

Reader review:

"Just finished Vicious Circle and understand now what people were raving about. It's truly a gripping read!"

Fratricide Unleashed

Fratricide Unleashed is the second book in the series and follows Jim McCormick to Belfast just as the campaigns of violence are concluding. McCormick makes it his primary goal to go after disgruntled Republicans who decide to continue their war. Again the shadowy hand of Military Intelligence is present as friends become enemies and former enemies become friends.

Reader review:

"What a compelling read! I wasn't able to put this book down. Full of twists and turns and though fiction, it was wholly believeable."

INTRODUCTION
Jim McCormick was a maverick policeman who served in Northern Ireland throughout the civil conflict that raged in his native country from 1970 until the late nineties.
In the first of the Steven Shannon trilogy of novels, Vicious Circle, we find McCormick in the East Londonderry / North Antrim area seeking to combat a Loyalist cell active in that area. In the second book, Fratricide Unleashed, we finf him having been transferred to Belfast where he hunts down disgruntled Republicans after the 1994 ceasefire.
In Killing McCormick, we find him being the hunted one instead of the hunter as Republicans set out to end his relentless pursuit of all paramilitaries from whichever quarter.


FOREWORD
Jim McCormick has dedicated his life to hunting down members of Loyalist and Republican paramilitary organisations. He became a hate figure for both so it was only a matter of time before someone decided that the time was ripe for revenge.

When he identified a known bomber in Belfast, McCormick embarked on a hunt that took him back to the northern counties. In order to protect their best bomber, senior Republicans decided it was time to take steps towards the ultimate aim of Killing McCormick ..........

# Contents

Chapter 1 ........................... 1

Chapter 2 ......................... 12

Chapter 3 ......................... 21

Chapter 4 ......................... 35

Chapter 5 ......................... 58

Chapter 6 ......................... 78

Chapter 7 ....................... 100

Chapter 8 ....................... 131

Chapter 9 ....................... 145

Chapter 10 ..................... 165

Chapter 11 ..................... 183

Chapter 12 ..................... 203

Epilogue ........................ 215

# Chapter 1

## *The stuff of nightmares*

The bomb exploded at 1.07am, exactly two minutes after the policemen entered the building. At 1.42 am, Detective Constable John Hargy was pronounced Dead on Arrival at the Royal Victoria Hospital in Belfast. His wife of two years fainted in the hospital corridor when she was told of her husband's death. At 1.54 am Detective Sergeant Jim McCormick heard the news and, for the first time in decades, he broke down and cried.

John Hargy would have been 46 years old had he lived another fortnight. He had been a policeman for twenty-three years, moving up the ranks from a rookie RUC constable to Detective Constable in CID. He had been a friend and confidant of Jim McCormick for twenty of those twenty-three years. From the first day they met, Hargy and McCormick had been friends. No one who knew them both could understand the friendship, though because Hargy was humorous, overt and a team player whereas McCormick had always been dour, reticent and a loner. The others used to ask them how long they had been married and if they were ever to divorce, which of them would get the house. Hargy used to laugh and join in the banter whilst McCormick seemed to simmer with resentment and rage at the jibes. Yet when it came to solving crimes, they were a dynamic pair.

They had not always worked together but they always kept in touch. Back in the old days, McCormick was a no-nonsense cop who seemed as familiar with every anecdote of criminal law as a good lawyer. He was certainly someone whom loved the law and believed firmly in it. He set himself up as an example to everyone and measured all other policemen by his own high standards. He progressed rapidly through the ranks and although his aloof personality was not endearing to his superiors, his success at solving crime in the most trying of circumstances was legendary. McCormick was nominally a Protestant but Loyalists involved in paramilitary activity were treated the same as Republicans. He was blind to the religion of those he arrested and as far as he was concerned they all served the same god: crime. He saw it as his calling to stamp out crime wherever he went and to bring everyone engaged in it to justice. When any of those he arrested wound up in court, McCormick would be there, staring silently at the defendant showing no emotion at all. If the accused was convicted he left the courtroom in the same manner as he did when they were released. Many believed his wife had left him because he was so devoid of emotion but

McCormick knew he had sacrificed his marriage by working long hours in the pursuit of wrong-doers. He understood that his wife could no longer bear the loneliness of those long shifts and felt she had no choice but to leave him in pursuit of a happier, more fulfilling life. He understood it and he could have prevented the breakdown of his marriage but policing was his first love and that was why he let her go. He was not the type to sandpaper door frames or paint the garden fence and find satisfaction in doing so. They were mundane tasks for someone lacking in imagination and that is what his wife wanted. Although he missed her at times and felt lonely sometimes, he had no regrets about her leaving. He was Jim McCormick the policeman, not Joe Bloggs the DIY fanatic.

After his wife left him, McCormick felt strangely liberated. He realised only then that he had been cautious and had held back in his quest to rid the country of paramilitaries. He reasoned that it had been down to a fear for her safety, a fear that his home might have been attacked resulting in harm coming her way. With her gone, he had nothing to lose, nothing to worry about. His war against terrorism only really begun then and he had no intention of allowing it to end. In many ways, Hargy held similar beliefs though he had the ability to carve up his life into distinct areas. He was an ardent cop who believed in the law and set out to be the scourge of terrorists and criminals. But he was also a committed husband and father who took time to play football with his young sons and take his wife out for meals. He holidayed at least once a year in a child friendly place where he seemed to illicit enjoyment from knowing his wife and children were enjoying themselves. He also played golf and squash with other officers and people who were not in the force. McCormick always found that strange, Hargy's need for companionship and to be a part of something. He lost count of the number of times Hargy had invited him to participate in these childish games but McCormick never accepted the invitations. He couldn't understand the appeal in batting a ball against a wall and then running about breathless trying to hit it again after the partner had smacked it. He wondered how anyone could find satisfaction in walking around a well-manicured hilly field striking a small ball with an iron stick in a bid to try to get it into a hole in the ground. He was baffled by the elation expressed by those who succeeded in the task. Yet that was Hargy and because he was such a good policeman, McCormick was always prepared to overlook his sporting follies.

They had served together in Belfast back when few wanted to be sitting ducks for terrorist guns. McCormick had no such qualms believing, like a good Presbyterian, that he wouldn't die a minute before his time. He didn't make it easy for the gunmen but he didn't hide from them either or try to curry favour with them the way some cops did. He noticed with contempt and disdain how some of his colleagues greeted these murderers by their first names and how they shared the occasional joke with each other. McCormick simply couldn't comprehend this kind of behaviour. These 'jokers' were the same people who were out trying to kill them and there they were, laughing and joking with them! Not Jim McCormick and, in fairness, not John Hargy either. Hargy was courteous but firm when he was bringing one of the animals to book. He never stepped out of line when searching a premises or questioning a suspect. He was a clever interrogator and had a fantastic memory for details that outstripped all who sat before him. Hargy used this talent to go over and over the same lines of questioning and when the suspect retold a detail differently, Hargy would pounce like a lion on a deer. McCormick envied this trait. He did not feel courteous when interviewing a suspect and he liked to hint and allege a lot to unnerve them as they sat there waiting for their solicitors to get them out. He did nothing illegal but he did enjoy playing mind games with them.

Everything was going great until that fateful day when they had gone to arrest Pearse Donoghue. It was a text book operation; maybe even a mundane one. McCormick was case hardened to searches and arrests and on that particular day he approached the operation with his customary thoroughness but with little enthusiasm. What happened wasn't his fault. He had gone by the book and found Donoghue in an upstairs bedroom. His orders to Donoghue were plain and unambiguous. He was to remain perfectly still and show his hands. What happened next had always been disputed and always would be but there was no dispute in McCormick's mind. Donoghue went for a gun and McCormick called out a warning before firing off enough rounds to prevent the terrorist from endangering the lives of others. OK, his actions caused the instant death of a Republican and sparked a riot in the Markets but he *had* saved the lives of his fellow officers. Not that that mattered to the Chief Constable who was more of a politician than a cop. Oh no, rather than show McCormick any gratitude, they had him packed off to Coleraine to investigate lost dogs and stolen lawnmowers. Of course all that changed with the killing spree that began in the County Londonderry area and its county Antrim hinterland. He had thrown himself into that and all along he had been dogged with interference from the London Calling boys. In the end, nearly all of the ones responsible for the killings were killed themselves. Two were shot dead by soldiers and a third was blown to pieces in his car in what was written off as a case of mistaken identity. A fourth suspect took off to England last he'd heard and the older man whom McCormick suspected of influencing the young killers ended up out of favour with his own organisation because of his dubious relationship with CID, namely himself. He was a chancer and McCormick hadn't wanted anything to do with him but he rationalised it along the lines that the end justifies the means...within reason, of course.

Now Jim McCormick was back in Belfast. After the

two Loyalists had been shot and a third blown up in County Londonderry, he had asked too many questions and ruffled too many feathers. It was one thing soliciting information from an informant but something else entirely to collude with a terrorist in the planning and execution of further crimes. McCormick had demanded to know the role played by shady army agents whom he sincerely believed were involved in the killing spree up there. Of course this had been met with stern opposition and before he knew it, he had been transferred back to Belfast and warned to let the matter drop. Back in the mayhem of trouble torn Belfast, that wasn't a problem as big Jim had his hands full from the moment he returned.

In all the time he had served in Coleraine, Jim had never lost touch with Hargy and he was delighted to be reunited with him once again on his return to the Capital. His superiors believed it best to reunite them as they were indeed a 'dynamic duo' and got excellent results when working together. Also, their different personalities somehow worked, especially in the interrogation rooms where they were able to play 'good cop, bad cop' quite naturally, confusing and bewildering the suspect and quite often resulting in a confession.

And now John Hargy was dead, blown to pieces by the IRA. They hadn't claimed it but it was obviously them. McCormick cried as one would cry over the death of a family member. Hargy wasn't a blood relative but he was a brother in another way, a more potent and meaningful way. After the shock had passed and his sorrow abated, McCormick went to the bathroom and washed his face as if washing away all of his grief and misery. He knew he should be making his way to the police station, if not the scene but he just couldn't think straight. His thoughts leapt from gross images of the bomb blast to memories of Hargy, laughing and telling jokes, to images of his wife and children, torn apart with grief just as their husband and father had been torn apart by that bomb. After ten torturous minutes, McCormick forced himself to have a shower and get dressed. He would go directly to the bomb site and then to the Hargy household. He was not emotionally equipped to provide comfort to grieving relatives and he knew it but he also knew Jenny Hargy knew it too. She would appreciate his calling and would understand his awkwardness. Once dressed, Jim McCormick drove at speed to the shop where pieces of his best and only friend lay scattered amongst the ruins.

Utter chaos met McCormick when he pulled up his car near the scene of the bomb. He flashed his badge at uniformed officers shivering in the cold February night and strode purposefully to the scene of the blast. He saw colleagues from the CID mingling with Scene of Crime officers. Ambulances were parked, their blue lights blinking silently and what seemed like dozens of uniformed personnel moved to and fro like a sea of blue and green. Two fire engines stood idly by, their job done and the crews stood chatting as the dust fell on them.

"This is a bad piece of work, Jim," the Detective Inspector said, stating the obvious. "No survivors at all. I know John was your friend so there's no need for you to be here. There are plenty of others who can take care of this. How are you bearing up?"

The Detective Inspector, John Greer, wasn't a friend of McCormick's. They had clashed many times over the years and Jim wasn't taken in by this show of concern. He knew Greer didn't want him there because this was personal. They, whoever 'they' were, had murdered his friend and McCormick had already determined that he would tear Belfast apart in his search for the culprits.

"Aye, it's the worst piece of work imaginable," he replied at length. "Anyone else besides John?"

"Another two uniformed constables, one of them only in a job less than a month. When the call came in, they were in the vicinity so they came straight here but waited. Hargy and Syd Boyce arrived ahead of the bomb disposal team. They were just to secure the area but it turns out that the call we got about the bomb was wrong; at least that's what we think. The call came in at 0030 hours and said there was a bomb in the first floor of the store timed to go off at 0130 hours. Well, Hargy thought he had a good half hour before it went off so he took the keys from the key holder and went inside to make sure there was no one about, night security and that type of thing. The thing is, the bomb went off at around 0107 hours, killing Hargy and the two young constables. Boyce was saved because he was outside speaking to the key holder and trying to move back the usual crowd of rubbernecking drunks. They're like moths to a light bulb at these things."

McCormick was stunned. "Hold on, sir! Are you telling me the caller *deliberately* gave the wrong time for the explosion? Someone actually gave the wrong time in order to take out anyone who arrived to secure the building?"

"Looks that way, Jim," Greer replied unmoved and emotionless. "That's what we're dealing with these days. It's not enough to commit murder. It has to be murder upon murder. We assumed this was one of these 'economic targets' they go on about, an English firm with a branch here. All part of their 'Brits Out' mantra. Turns out it was that and more. They destroy an English company and kill three cops to boot. Evil scum!"

McCormick stared past Greer to the carnage behind him. The Provos had lured John here to kill him. They didn't care about the shop or the economic impact of blowing it up. The whole reason behind this was to kill cops. Hargy went in there like a lamb to the slaughter! He never stood a chance.

"Go home, Jim," the Detective Inspector advised. "There are plenty here to sort out this mess tonight.

It's in the morning we need you and every morning hereafter to nail the scum who did this. Away you go now and get some sleep. We will need fresh heads to get to the bottom of this."

McCormick paused for a time and didn't notice Greer walking over to the other police men and women to issue orders and organise the personnel. All Jim could see was the broken glass, dust, bricks, torn clothes and carnage of what was once a fine department store that employed many and sold their goods at affordable prices. Now it was a tomb that held what was left of John Hargy and the two constables. He shook his head in a mixture of disbelief and horror. Now it was time to go and see Jenny and her children. This will be even worse than what I have seen this night, McCormick thought as he drove in the direction of their home.

## Chapter 2

### *The Aftermath*

Many people thought Jim McCormick incapable of emotion, including those who had known him all his life. That's if it was possible to *really* know McCormick. At primary school he had been an awkward boy who seemingly saw no need to befriend his classmates and although acknowledged as a bright pupil who paid attention in class and completed his home-works faithfully, he demonstrated few social skills. When his classmates played tig and rounders, Jim was happy to walk around the football pitch or playground alone, lost in his thoughts. He was described by his teachers as quietly confident but withdrawn. He would be described in this fashion by many for the rest of his life.

Grammar school brought no real changes to his personality but many remembered his stubborn ability on the rugby pitch. He had been tall for his age and something of a fitness fanatic with a love of running and non-team sports. Those who attended grammar school with McCormick recall that although he was a member of the rugby team every year, he was never a team player. They remembered how he hated to pass the ball and would prefer to lose the play than pass to a safe player. He seldom missed receiving a pass but when he did he invariably blamed the other player. However, one thing that also stood out in their minds was that McCormick never held a grudge. He said his piece and did what he believed was right and that was all there was to it.

The Jim McCormick that awoke from a short nap the night his friend, one of the few people he would ever call a friend, John Hargy was blown to little pieces by an IRA bomb, was the same Jim McCormick. He awoke alone and stared at his reflection in the mirror for a good five minutes before resolving that he would leave no stone unturned until he had the murderers of his friend behind bars. He resented the fact that they would be treated like heroes by the community and fellow prisoners. He regretted that they would not be sent to the gallows for their crimes but McCormick had long ago steeled himself to ignore the injustices of the justice system. He regarded his role now as the one who rounded them up and let others live with the consequences of giving them easy prison time. This gave McCormick a crystal clear conscience.

On the way to the station, McCormick thought about the uncontrolled grief and despair he had witnessed a few hours previously when he sat trying, in his own awkward way, to console Jenny Hargy. He had been embarrassed and annoyed at the crying and wailing that came straight from Jenny's heart. He couldn't explain either emotion and felt guilty at being embarrassed and annoyed. He should have felt empathy and sympathy but he hadn't and that angered him. However, the look of pure misery on Jenny's face convinced him that bringing her man's killers to justice wasn't his job; it would be his mission. As he parked his car he went further. It would now be his mission in life to destroy the killers and the organisations they thrived in. OK, so that had always been his aim, but now it was his *mission*.

As he walked to his desk, his colleagues nodded briefly at him and a few of the braver ones patted him on the arm. Jim McCormick wasn't the type to mollycoddle or sympathise with, regardless of the circumstances. McCormick nodded back and then pulled out a sheaf of papers and pretended to study the contents. In reality, all he could think of was his friend John. He didn't see the remains of his friend after the explosion but he had created an image that was horrific but now inescapable. In his mind's eye, John Hargy was killed again and again and again without end. The shrill ring from his desk phone snapped McCormick out of his morbid day dreams. Only then did he realise that he had scrunched a page up tight in his fist. He discarded the page and answered the phone. It was Greer.

"Morning Jim, how are you?"

"Fine sir," was the only reply Jim could muster.

"Look, Jim, I don't believe that you're 'fine', Greer replied, oozing concern. "If you need some time off, that won't be a problem."

"I am good," McCormick replied briefly. "I don't need time off. I need to work. We are a man down after last night. A good man, too."

"Quite. Well, Jim, it is very important that we find the culprits and we will leave no stone unturned until we do. However, it may be unwise for you to be a part of that investigation. I feel you may have been too close to Hargy and it might affect your judgement. I am sure you can see the wisdom in this."

McCormick took the receiver from his ear and stared at it as if it had just bit him. He felt the rage rise from his feet and settle just behind his eyes. Greer isn't one bit concerned about me, McCormick thought angrily. He's trying to cover his own ass here and he knows I will tear through the Provos like a hot knife through butter! There had been rumours about talks between the government and Republicans and Greer was always pandering to the politicians. McCormick brought the receiver back to his ear.

"I am fine , sir, and I feel I have plenty to contribute to the investigation. I don't mind if I am not leading it but I *do* want to be on it. I believe my close professional relationship with John Hargy would actually be a benefit, not a problem," he replied stiffly. His reply was met with silence.

At length Greer replied. "OK, Jim, I will get back to you."

McCormick replaced the receiver and looked around

the room as if everyone had heard the conversation with Greer. No one had and no one paid him any attention. Outside the room, through the glass, he spotted John McCrum, a recently promoted Detective Constable only out of uniform a few months. McCormick rose quickly from his chair and made a beeline for McCrum, placing himself directly in front of him.

"Are you on the Hargy case?" he asked without any introduction or small talk.

McCrum gave him a measured look and nodded silently.

"Who's the Sergeant in charge?" McCormick demanded of his junior.

"Felix Bryson", McCrum answered quickly, hoping that McCormick would leave him alone. He didn't know McCormick personally but a colleague reaching retirement had warned McCrum to avoid McCormick if he wanted to see retirement someday. He had added that one sure way of getting killed was to stick close to McCormick. McCrum had been intrigued by this towering, stern-faced cop in front of him but had managed to remain intrigued from a safe distance. He didn't even realise that McCormick *knew* him yet here he was, less than two feet away, demanding answers which McCrum gave quickly.

"Bryson won't try too hard," McCormick said gruffly. "He is nothing more than Greer's messenger boy and he won't even turn a page in his notebook with Greer's OK. Did you know John Hargy?"

"Knew him to see," McCrum replied quietly. "Came across to me as a good chap and a good police officer. I would like to see whoever done it in here breaking a lot of sweat."

McCormick stared at McCrum for what seemed to the latter to be an hour but was really only two minutes.

"Look, here's the thing," McCormick began, grabbing McCrum by the arm and walking him towards the main doors. "They won't let me on the case and not because I am a bad detective. I suspect it's more like the fact that I'm a *good* detective! The politicians own Greer and he might not try too hard to catch the culprits if his political masters don't want him to upset the Provos. So, basically, I am out of the loop. What I need is a man on the inside; a man who will take advice and keep me posted. I am wondering if you are that man?"

McCrum felt that the big detective wasn't so much *asking* if he was the man or *telling* him that he was the man. As McCormick stood expectantly before him, McCrum considered his options and concluded quickly that he only had one option. He needed to play for time to work out how this was going to pan out.

"How about you and me having a cup of tea and

seeing how that might work?" McCrum suggested hopefully. "It's a big ask, especially if Greer is against you knowing anything. I am not refusing you but we would need to box clever. Fair enough?"

McCormick nodded briefly and they made arrangements to meet at McCormick's home that night to discuss the matter further. For the rest of the day, McCormick suffered the indignity of watching other detectives speaking to each other in whispers, casting him furtive glances in case he might be listening to them. McCormick endured this for as long as he felt he could before deciding to get some fresh air.

"Well!" he announced, "I must get going. There might be cat burglars to catch or maybe some old woman's pet cat has ran away. You know it is, folks! A cop's work is never done!"

He slammed the door hard as he left the main office, not looking back in case the sight of the shocked and uneasy faces of his colleagues would only add to his frustration and anger. As he strode out of the building, McCormick's thoughts turned to John Hargy. Pausing at the railings to the side of the building, he gripped the top so tightly that his knuckles turned white. He tormented himself by imagining Hargy's last hours, last minutes and last seconds. His head told him it was a pointless exercise but his heart wouldn't let him escape from the horror of his old friend's dying moments. Who did it? McCormick wondered. He tried to recall the name of every bomb maker in Belfast and the surrounding area and resolved to get the information he needed one way or another.

It was late when McCormick pulled up two streets away from McCrum's home. He had no intention of implicating himself or his new found ally (he hoped) by brazenly parking outside his home. A lifetime of service in the police told Jim that sometimes he needed to be as wary of his own colleagues as anyone else. He walked cautiously to the back door as agreed and, after the necessary security precautions had been observed, McCrum opened the door and let his superior officer into his home.

"Well, have you given the idea any more thought?" McCormick asked without any of the customary niceties people expect.

McCrum nodded. He had given the suggestion a *lot* of thought and had spent a lot of the day seeking to find out more about this abrupt detective and their boss, John Greer. He had found out that McCormick wasn't a popular policeman on account of his brusque manner and his seeming inability to form friendships within the force, Hargy having been a notable exception. However, on balance, he also found no one who could say anything negative about him as a cop, just as a human. Most regarded him as more like a policeman from a TV series than a real cop with his impeccable dress, abrupt manner, incorruptible nature and his determination to always act within the law he had sworn to uphold. Indeed, he had become a byword and a cliché. McCrum discovered that if a colleague was acting in a quiet and withdrawn manner, he or she was "having a McCormick day" or if someone was over reacting over a petty issue, they were "being a McCormick". It seemed to McCrum that this strange police man was probably a model cop and for that reason, others were wary of him and sought to avoid him because it was impossible to meet his bar. He had also discovered that Greer was pretty much as McCormick had described him. He was a friend of the politicians and civil servants but not necessarily a friend to his officers. The common belief seemed to be that Greer would direct policing policy in a way that suited political mandarins and the men in grey he dined with so often, as opposed to conventional policing which his officers sought in vain. Greer was a close friend of the Chief Constable and it was rumoured that he spent more time at Stormont Castle than in any police station.

All of these things brought McCrum to a conclusive decision; he would help McCormick.

## Chapter 3

### *Partners*

After half an hour of conversation, mainly McCormick doing the talking, McCrum's wife, Alison, came into the dining room with tea, coffee and biscuits which met with the approval of the largely teetotal McCormick.

"You're not a drinker then?" he demanded, stating it more than asking. "I don't trust folk who drink. They talk too much. Believe me, John, drink has seen more folk in jail and more cops kicked out of the job than you might imagine. A hot half for the flu or one as a nightcap and that's my limit."

"I can drink a beer now and then but never enough to get drunk," McCrum admitted warily. "It's been years since I had more than just a couple."

McCormick nodded his approval and they continued to make their plans. They agreed that McCrum would bring McCormick's suggestions to the table, passing them off as his own, and he would keep Jim informed of how the case was progressing or otherwise. The first thing McCormick wanted to know was what plans were in place for arresting the usual suspects, known bomb makers, people who planted bombs and so on. McCrum conceded that he wasn't aware of any such plans but he was confident that that step would be taken very soon. McCormick ordered his host to get paper and a pen and then dictated the names and addresses of suspects with clarity and rapidity as McCrum struggled to write down the details being fired at him. They discussed other matters including the vital report giving the details of the type of bomb. McCormick explained to an already aware McCrum that many bombers leave a kind of 'signature' in that specific bomb makers tend to construct all of their bombs in the same way, unique to themselves. Thereby, the theory goes, one could have a good idea of who made the bomb by examining the *type* of bomb.

When McCormick left, John McCrum slumped in his favourite armchair in the spacious living room and considered the conversation – *conspiracy* – he had just been involved in. Alison entered the room with a brandy and sat down opposite him on the sofa.

"He seems like a nice chap," she offered, referring to McCormick.

"He's definitely a one-off," her husband replied. "It's a good job he didn't see that brandy though. He would have lost all faith in me, it seems. I don't know, Alison. Is it possible to be as straight as that? He's like a robot! I don't doubt his commitment and his dedication but I'm not sure he's even human!"

"Will you be able to work with him OK? At least he came around for a chat and made the effort to get to know you," Alison opined.

"Aye, that's true", McCrum replied. If only she knew, he thought grimly.

Next morning John McCrum busied himself researching the information McCormick had given him the previous evening. Armed with a list of potential suspects, McCrum spent two hours rifling through files of convicted and suspected Republican bombers. The IRA had claimed responsibility for the bombing so he concentrated his efforts in looking for members of that organisation only. He had eight suspects and soon he had gathered so many files he needed a small trolley to transport them from the records section to his own desk. A team meeting had been called for eleven o'clock and it was 10.30am by the time McCrum had his load of files stacked on the floor beside his paper covered desk. He examined the list again and tried to commit the names on it to memory. There would obviously be questions as to how he, a junior detective, could possibly know who might be responsible. They would wonder how he had been able to come up with a list of names so quickly. But, true to form, McCormick had thought about that and advised McCrum to speak to colleagues before the meeting at different times, asking them who they thought may have been responsible. McCormick reasoned that his junior could then plausibly produce his list and claim the names came from conversations with older colleagues and that he had simply recorded what they had told him. McCrum felt it was strange, all this cloak-and-dagger nonsense but he knew

McCormick was indeed a strange man and caution of this kind was his trademark.

The meeting was chaired by Detective Sergeant Felix Bryson and was not at all what McCrum had expected. There was no brainstorming, no pooling of ideas and no obvious enthusiasm from the other detectives present for catching the murderers of their late colleague. Instead, Bryson dealt with ordinary and mundane matters, labouring over things that seemed insignificant and unimportant. The detectives present agreed amongst themselves who would be attending Hargy's funeral the next day and then came the issue of his murder. Again, Bryson seemed devoid of emotion as he summarised what they knew, including a preliminary report from the coroner, the SOCO leader and useless statements taken from witnesses who, in reality, had seen nothing at all of any significance. The subject then turned to likely suspects and as names were suggested, the detectives made notes. Three of those on McCrum's list were named but after a short time the conversation seemed to dry up. McCrum hesitated before raising his hand warily as an indication that he wished to speak. He was suddenly aware that none of the others had done this and felt like a child seeking the attention of his teacher. Bryson looked at him and nodded, letting him know he had permission to speak.

"Well, the thing is, you see," McCrum stammered, "I have been speaking to a number of colleagues yesterday and today and I have a list here of likely suspects. Three from this list have been named already here but there's five more I have been given. John O'Kane, Frank McHugh, Jack McDevitt, Damien McShane and Barney Duffin."

Bryson looked at McCrum without speaking and then turned to Detective Constable Harry Houston his confidant and close friend. He didn't speak to Houston either but raised his eyebrows as if seeking him to confirm McCrum's suggestions or otherwise. Houston moved uncomfortably in his seat as if sitting in a different position would give him some kind of clarity.

"Well, yes, it would make good sense to include those names on a list of possible suspects," he said slowly. "They have reputations as bomb makers or at least that is what our intelligence suggests. I would be interested to know where you got those names though," he added, looking at McCrum.

"I can't remember who gave which names." McCrum replied blithely.

"They sound like names Jim McCormick might suggest," Bryson observed, turning again to stare hard at McCrum. "I must make it crystal clear that Detective Sergeant McCormick is *not* involved in this case in any way. Perhaps you didn't know that, John?"

"I think I know who you mean," McCrum replied

nonchalantly. "I don't believe I have spoken to him yet except to say 'hello' in passing. Might I ask why he is not involved in the case? I am told he and Detective Hargy were quite close."

Bryson looked at the pad on his desk and then scanned the room, glancing at each of his colleagues before turning his attention to McCrum again.
"Yes, you *might* ask indeed, even though you have answered your own question. McCormick and Hargy *were* close and therein lies the problem. McCormick isn't objective at the best of times and the close nature of his relationship with Hargy rules him out as useful. I don't think I would be shocking anyone here if I said that Jim McCormick is a very single-minded man who can be a trail at the best of times and his personality does not lend itself to be productive in this particular case where certain sensitivities are called for."

Noting the silence, Houston felt obliged to simplify things a tad.

"What Felix means," he explained, "is that Jim is like a bull in a china shop at the best of times and with Hargy being his mate as well as his colleague, he would be even worse than usual. He would be ripping everyone with a Celtic top out of their beds at dawn and Castlereagh and Gough put together wouldn't hold them! Then Sinn Fein would be on every TV channel and in every newspaper crying 'police brutality' and there would be riots in the streets! Some of us remember when Jim blew away a Republican during a raid before. The suspect died and the city went up in flames. Greer isn't going to risk that happening again. There! I said what Felix here felt he couldn't say! Am I right?"

"Quite," Bryson said nodding. "Jim can be quite a handful when he starts and he won't listen to reason or think of the consequences of his actions. The Chief wants him excluded from this case and so do I. So, no whispering or slipping him notes. Jim's out."

As a thick silence enveloped the room, McCrum considered his next move. He felt an inexplicable urge to defend McCormick whom he barely knew yet he had committed himself to keeping him in the loop so he didn't want to arouse Bryson's suspicions by pressing the matter. Bryson broke the silence.

"Are we clear, McCrum?" he demanded. McCrum pursed his lips and nodded as if he naturally agreed to withhold information from the maverick McCormick.

When the meeting ended, McCrum returned to his mountain of files. He found it hard to concentrate as he reflected on his first real "team meeting". Bryson and Houston seemed definitely more paranoid about McCormick and the need to exclude him from all enquiries than actually making a start on finding out who murdered McCormick. He was mulling over this when Houston approached his desk and asked him to join him for a coffee. Suspiciously, McCrum followed Houston, shuffling past the other desks and detectives, his arms hanging by his sides as he walked. At school, his classmates had nicknamed McCrum "the Gorilla" because of his lacklustre manner of walking in this fashion but his lay look hid a sharp and calculating mind. As such, he didn't react when Houston practically ordered him to bring the coffees from the counter whilst the Detective Constable took a seat at a table in the corner.

"We haven't really had the chance to get to know each other," Houston stated as McCrum sat down opposite him with the hot drinks. "In a station as busy as this, we seldom have the time to meet socially or strike up a friendship," he added, smiling apologetically.

McCrum nodded, waiting for Houston to continue. It was the right move as it was clear that Houston was determined to dominate the conversation.

"I suppose you might be wondering why Felix was so adamant that big McCormick must be kept out of the Hargy investigation. Well, you can't really understand where Felix was coming from without knowing the kind of person McCormick is. He's a one-off, that's for sure! Put it this way, if I was in a tight spot, he is the one man I would want beside me. The only thing is that it would probably have been McCormick who got me into the tight spot in the first place! He's just over-zealous, I suppose; the kind of person who bends but never breaks the rules. He's also a mass of contradictions because he seems to despise Special Branch and the running of agents yet he has his own touts and contacts. I suppose the difference with McCormick's touts is that he won't protect them. He will milk them dry and bully and browbeat them if he has something hanging over them but if he catches any of them breaking the law or telling him a lie, he will have them lifted and locked up in the blink of an eye."

"None of these sound like negatives to me," McCrum ventured. "And nothing you have said explains the obvious hostility Bryson showed this morning."

Houston moved in his seat. "Well, that's what some might think but the fact is that Jim has a knack of upsetting apple carts. Like it or not, touts save lives and now and again we have to turn a blind eye to some of their activities. Not Jim, though! He hounds them down and locks them up so then they refuse to cooperate with us and we lose intelligence. You see, Jim never sees the big picture! Another thing is, he isn't attuned to political moves and changes. Yes we have to keep law and order, but we have to do it with an eye on what's happening politically. Do you see where I am coming from?"

"I would appreciate it if you would speak a bit more clearly," McCrum replied, knowing full well what was being implied but wanting Houston to say it.

"Right," Houston began resolutely, "things are

changing politically and it looks like the Provos are considering calling a ceasefire. Now, I don't mean a break; I mean a total end to their violence! Now we have to police the country with this in mind. We don't want to give them an excuse to change their mind about the ceasefire. We want to *encourage* them to end it. Now, try telling Jim McCormick that! Firstly, he wouldn't believe it. Secondly, he would have a fit at the thought of us taking our boots off the necks of the Provos! He might only be one man but he could do a lot of damage. It's not that we don't *like* Jim or that we don't *trust* him. We just can't really control him. He is a very hard-headed man and subtlety is lost on him. The peace moves are lost on him and it's cool heads we need at the minute. Is that any clearer?"

McCrum nodded thoughtfully. "Aye that does indeed clear things up a bit. But can we really trust the Provos? What if they're at their work? They are talking peace, you say, but they are still killing policemen."

Houston sighed as if exasperated at McCrum's apparent inability to grasp the subtleties of politics.

"I am not in a position to tell you how much we know but it's suffice to say we have intelligence oozing out of the Provos. OK, so we don't know every operation they will engage in but we have successfully penetrated them to an extent whereby we know what their plans are, their political agenda, if you like. Trust me, you will soon be able to sleep with your door open if what we have been told is correct and I have no reason to doubt the information we have been receiving. The hawks within the Republican movement have been marginalised and neutered. It is now controlled by doves and even the former hard-liners are loyal to them. They are beaten and they know it. It's just a matter of them extracting themselves from their 'war' without losing face. That process has been ongoing for quite some time now and the outcome will certainly be a ceasefire. We simply *can't* rock the boat or allow the Jim McCormicks of this world to rock it either."

McCrum studied the empty cup before him, trying to process everything he had just heard. There was no doubt about it; the hierarchy of the police force he was a part of were being controlled by political developments taking place behind closed doors. The message here was clear, too; investigate the IRA by all means but make it a half-hearted effort and do not in any way provoke them. Given that his colleagues were still being murdered by the same Republicans, this would not be easy and for some, undoubtedly like Jim McCormick, impossible. He nodded slightly as he came to the conclusion that policing was now being dictated by political manoeuvres and that politicians would be directing the Chief Constable, not events on the ground. Houston, however, took this slight nodding as a sign of agreement and understanding on the part of his colleague and smiled broadly at him.

"Good man, John! I knew you would understand the complexities of the current situation and that this is something Jim wouldn't be able to comprehend or grasp. It's not ideal, but it has to be done and you know what they say; 'ours is not to question why ....'"

'They' aren't cops, McCrum thought sullenly. 'They' aren't burying their friends and comrades. Although he didn't know exactly what he could or would do, John McCrum knew one thing; he was going to help Jim McCormick as much as he could because if the conversation he had just had told him anything it was that there actually were good cops and bad cops and that the good were being painted bad and the bad ones were in control.

"I understand fully," McCrum said at length, looking Houston in the eye. "Jim McCormick would be a liability in this new departure. Thanks for helping me understand."

Houston was blushing and shaking his head, rising from his seat and telling McCrum that he was no political genius but that he was delighted to have been of some assistance. With that he left the canteen and left McCrum to his thoughts. Now it wasn't a question of *if* he should brief McCormick but when. That very evening, he decided. Jim will be livid!

When he met McCormick that night, McCrum was surprised at his colleague's reaction. McCormick periodically shook his head, grimaced and grit his teeth but there were no loud outbursts and no losing control.

"This doesn't surprise me," McCormick said evenly when McCrum had finished his account of the chat with Houston. "The big chiefs are always hand-picked because of their political savvy, not their policing ability. They are there to do the bidding of the men in suits but of course if I were to say that publicly, I would be written off as a head case! I thought when they excluded me from the investigation there was more to it than just me being close to Hargy. Houston is just a lackey; it's Greer and Bryson I have the problem with! They are in the paymasters' pockets and they will do their dirty best to ruin the likes of me! Are you still game to help me, John?"

"I am here, aren't I?" McCrum replied quietly. "I can see what's happening, Jim, but in order to help you, I need to convince them that I have little more than a passing contact with you. If they think for a moment I am in cahoots with you, they will either put me off the case or put me back in uniform and I like this suit."

McCormick laughed briefly at McCrum's dry wit. This dull cop might just be the man he needed, McCormick thought as he stared at McCrum. He's a shapeless and hapless looking chap but maybe that's what's needed. Who will ever suspect this character of anything more than reading files? When

McCrum caught McCormick's stare, the latter looked away as if hiding his thoughts from his colleague. Unlikely as it may seem, this could be an unlikely but very successful partnership.

## Chapter 4

### A Blast from the Past

Within a week, McCormick had other things to think about. Gunmen had opened fire on a foot patrol on Divis Street and two constables had been seriously wounded. Although they lacked enthusiasm, Greer and Bryson had little choice but to give the investigation to McCormick. No one had died in the attack and the injuries the policemen had received were not life-threatening. They reasoned that McCormick would not tear Belfast apart when no one had died though Bryson made a point of sitting him down and warning him that he expected McCormick to act responsibly. He even offered a veiled threat should the zealous McCormick act too rashly in pursuit of his enquiries.

McCormick went directly to Musgrave Hospital to interview the two victims of the gun attack, fully in the knowledge that there was nothing they could tell him. These incidents were always the same; masked gun men open fire from a passing car or they pop up out of nowhere, open fire and then jump into a waiting car and take off. No one gets an accurate description of them and the car is set on fire within minutes of the incident. Yet procedure dictated that his first port of call was the two injured policemen.

McCormick interviewed each of the Constables in

turn and, as expected, there weren't able to help. They had been walking a short distance when they heard a car screeching to a halt. Before they could react, a gunman opened fire wounding them both. As they fell, they heard the car door slam and saw the car taking off. The car was a navy coloured Volkswagen Polo but McCormick already knew that as it had been found burnt out about a mile from the shooting. When he pressed them for a description of the gunman, all they could tell him was that he appeared to be of slim build and around five feet ten inches tall. He had worn a balaclava so they couldn't help with a facial description or hair colour. McCormick left the hospital no wiser but not disappointed as he had expected no more.

As he drove to the station, McCormick considered his options. The car had been burnt out near Divis flats and the gun man was tall and thin. Not much to go on but McCormick decided to use the lack of information to his advantage. When he got to his desk, McCormick busied himself checking all of the suspected IRA members in the vicinity of where the car had been burned, looking for any who might be described as tall and thin. After a few hours, he had narrowed the original list down to three suspects who fitted the bill. Photographs of Terence Doyle, Seamus Reilly and Brendan McBride stared back at McCormick from his desk. All tall, all thin. 'Pull throughs!' he snorted with derision. I must sweat a few more pounds off these toe-rags even though they could do with putting more on. He lifted the files and strode purposefully into Bryson's office to seek permission for the arrest warrants.

"Your grounds for the arrest of these men?" Bryson asked, peering over the files at McCormick.

"They fit the witnesses descriptions and they live in the vicinity of where the car was found, sir! McCormick replied stiffly. "Also, they have form. McBride has served time for possession of firearms and the other two have cropped up in Intel reports as having been involved in gun attacks."

Bryson didn't reply immediately but instead spent a few minutes reading the files on the three suspects. He looked like he was trying to decide what to do before looking directly at McCormick.

"OK. We will bring them in and I will secure the warrants. Now hear me out, Jim. I know you aren't happy about not being part of the Hargy investigation but you must understand that policing is changing. I can't go into detail but we can't go charging into Divis like it's 'Gunfight at the OK Corral'. We need to make sure that we remove these people from their homes with the minimum of fuss and as quickly as possible, We don't want to antagonise the other residents of the area by staying too long and preventing them from going about their daily business."

"Well, sir, with all due respect, the arrests will be made at six in the morning. I don't expect too many residents will be up at that hour. In fact, if it was four hours later, the majority of them would still be in their beds."

Bryson twitched and then slapped his desk hard with his hand. "This is why there are problems between me and you, McCormick! What kind of a comment is that? It's a generalisation of the worst kind and the type of attitude that creates more problems for us. There are plenty of good people in and around Divis and we should only be targetting the few rotten apples who lurk there like leeches, feeding off the backs of their long-suffering neighbours!"

McCormick didn't flinch. "Maybe then we shouldn't bother arresting these three, sir. By the sound of things their neighbours will be jamming our phone lines with information about who's responsible. If there as good as you believe, that is, sir."

"Get out of my office!" Bryson exploded. "You will be accompanied by Detective Constable Houston and although you are the senior officer, you will wait with the transport and allow Houston to make the arrests! That, McCormick, is an order!"

"Very good, sir, I will protect the cars," McCormick replied, turning swiftly and leaving the claustrophobic office as his boss muttered angrily and incoherently behind him. When he entered the main office, the other detectives had clearly heard the raised voice of their boss and looked warily at McCormick. He smiled broadly at them.

"Not a good time to ask for a pay rise or the rest of the day off," he breezed. "The boss is very emotional and needs time alone, I think."

The detectives looked at each other and whispered, glancing cautiously Bryson's office door. Houston came over to McCormick's desk.

"A bad meeting, Jim?" he ventured.

"No, not really. I got the green light to scoop these three characters," he said, showing Houston the files. "And the good news for you is that you just got promotion! You are the chosen one; chosen by Bryson to slap the cuffs on them. My job will be to valet the cars. Well, I'm sure he will fill you in. I'm off to meet a contact. See you here at five in the morning, Harry!"

After a brief phone call, McCormick set off to meet his contact. This was a necessary evil as far as Jim was concerned; meeting a Republican to glean information. He despised his handful of contacts and was careful to refer to them as just that: contacts. McCormick totally disagreed with the concept of informers and agents and his treatment of his contacts was not at all like the relationships he knew existed between paid informers and agents and their handlers in Special Branch and the Intelligence Services. Oh yes, he had heard all the arguments! Highly placed agents passing on vital information; lives being saved; turning a blind eye to the odd crime in order to net bigger fish. It just wasn't within

McCormick's make up to allow anyone a free reign or to live outside the law. He didn't mind catching a criminal committing a minor infraction and using it against them but that was it! He would pump them for information but should they get caught in a criminal act, they were on their own. The contact he was meeting tonight was Joe McNamee, in McCormick's opinion, a particularly odious young man but, he shrugged as he drove, sometimes you just have to play the hand you're dealt.

Joe McNamee replaced the telephone receiver and slammed his hand against the wall. McCormick! How he hated that sneering cop! He stood sullenly recollecting their first meeting two years before and grimaced. There had been a robbery which he had been involved in on behalf of the Movement. McNamee's job had been to stash the money safely away after being counted and McNamee and his fellow robbers each shared the knowledge that they had netted almost fifteen thousand pounds. After the three had counted the money, McNamee had left with the haul and was walking briskly to the hiding place when a police car cut him off and a tall, stern looking detective steeped out and grabbed him. McNamee remembered how the big cop had bundled him into the car and, along with another policeman, they had taken him to a car park on the outskirts of Belfast. They had pulled McNamee out of the car and searched him, finding the cash in seconds. The other cop, Hargy, who had been killed lately by a bomb, flipped through the bundles of notes which the robbers had collated in thousand pound bundles. It didn't take long to establish that there was around fifteen thousand pounds in the bag.

"Don't tell me," McCormick had said, mockingly, "You have been saving up to buy a new boat and you were just heading to the docks to make your purchase!"

"Or maybe you had all of this in a shoe box below your bed and decided to take it somewhere safer like the back of a hedge or maybe a plant pot somewhere?" Hargy had speculated laughing.

"Or maybe you just knocked over a place tonight along with two other toe rags and you were just on your way to hide the loot?" McCormick had said menacingly.

McNamee remembered the shock he felt along with the confusion. What was going on? Why had these two policemen taken him to the car park and gone on with that charade? How had they known what had just happened. And then it dawned on him! He had been set up! Someone had tipped these two off and they had waited to grab him and bring him here. But why?

"How much did you say is there, John?" McCormick asked his smiling colleague.

"Oh somewhere in the region of fifteen grand," Hargy replied happily.

"How about this," McCormick began, staring intently at the unfortunate McNamee."We will not book you for this. In fact, we will take you back to where we picked you up but we'll hold onto the stash. In a day or two we will release a statement to say we found it and name the business you took it from. So far so good? OK, I will assume you're following the story. So we release our statement only we will say we recovered *ten grand.* My guess is your mates know how much you took; it wasn't in neat bundles when you took it so I am assuming you all sat and counted it. Well, can you imagine the consequences? Your mates will run squealing to the Provos that there was fifteen grand and we will say, No, it was only ten. Then the Nutting Squad will be called in to ask you a few serious questions about the missing five grand. By the time they're through with you, you will have admitted stealing the missing five grand and you will likely have admitted killing Trotsky with an ice pick over Mexico way! How's that for a plan, Joe?"

Standing in the hallway two years later McNamee remembered only too vividly how he had panicked. He remembered how McCormick and Hargy had chatted to each other, speculating how long he would last at the hands of Internal Security and the degrees of torture he would have to endure. He knew they were right. He wouldn't be able to stand it and he would admit stealing the money, even though he hadn't. They would kill him!

"Ever see them pictures of the bodies and the bags over their heads on a border road, Joe?" McCormick had asked. "A lonely death indeed. Awful for the family; how do you think your old ma will take that, Joe? Would it kill her?"

Before Joe got back into the car that fateful night, he had agreed to work for McCormick. He had begged to be allowed to hand over the cash but the big cop refused point blank. He had reached Joe two £20 notes but then quickly snatched them back.

"You will tell us where you are for hiding this lot," McCormick insisted, "and we will find it in a day or two. If we are too late, so be it, but we will be out looking for it. As for these two £20 notes, we will hold onto them as insurance. Your fingerprints are on them and we will trace them back to the robbery and you are for jail, son. Have we a deal?"

McNamee hid the stash where he told McCormick it would be and the very next morning he nervously went back and removed a £20 note with a gloved hand, leaving it lying where the rest had been. He took the rest of the haul and quickly handed it over to the local IRA commander. When he next met McCormick, the big cop had smiled wryly, telling him they had searched the hiding place and found the £20 note. He hadn't asked where the rest went or if McNamee had moved it. It was irrelevant; McCormick had a double Ace in the form of the two £20 notes which could get McNamee seven years at best. And now McCormick was demanding to see him! He pulled on his coat and trudged to the designated meeting place with the greatest possible reluctance.

"Hello, Joe, what do you know?" McCormick asked poetically when McNamee got into the car.

"What do you want to know?" McNamee asked nervously. "If it's about Hargy, I don't know anything. Away out of my league."

"No, nothing to do with that," McCormick replied, looking straight ahead. "I want to know about Doyle, McBride and Reilly, all neighbours of yours and all part of Ireland's Finest".

McCormick's sarcasm and cocky attitude had always irked McNamee who believed that the cop's general air of superiority and disdain epitomised everything that his community found hateful about the police.

"I know them but I am not in a position to know much about them," McNamee said carefully. "They're shooters and don't really mix with people like me."

"You know, I am really impressed with the security structures you boys have in place," McCormick said loudly. "Like, no matter what name I throw at you, you know nothing about them! I am also surprised because it's no secret that Special Branch and the Military Intelligence boys practically run your leadership even though you're too stupid or naïve to believe it!" He sighed deeply as if disappointed. "OK, so tell me what you *do* know about these three scumbags."

"Well, like I say, they are shooters and they keep themselves to themselves. Reilly and McBride live alone in the Tower and Doyle lives with a girl from Twinbrook. They aren't bombers, though. Just guns."

McCormick pursed his lips and frowned as if considering this information.

"Well if that's all you have then we're done here," he said dismissively. "Out you get and fight for your Socialist Republic where, by the way, you will be expected to work for a living. You need to make a point of finding out more about this thing you're in or I will have to think about cashing in them two £20 notes some time soon."

McNamee got out of the car angrily and headed home. Who did McCormick think he was? And how much longer will h go on about that £40? It's OK for him, sitting in his office in his crisp suit. If I come across as nosey or asking about things I shouldn't, I will draw attention to myself and end up on that border road anyway! McCormick! What an utter scumbag!

At five o'clock the next morning, the police station was buzzing with activity. McCormick conferred briefly with Houston, telling him the living arrangements of the three suspects before they set off to make their arrests. They left the station in a convoy, a mix of land rovers and cars and quickly found themselves at Divis flats. As ordered by Bryson, Houston led the raiding parties whilst McCormick waited with the vehicles on the roadside. It took about an hour to extract two of the three suspects and McCormick muttered angrily as Houston came towards him with Doyle and McBride.

"Just two, Harry?" McCormick asked, genuinely surprised.

"Aye, the third bird has flown. Maybe stayed with a mate, a woman or whatever. His flat is lived in and the date on the milk is tomorrow so he must have just decided to stay wherever he was last night. We can have a look for him later. He will need to get himself a joiner anyway; when he didn't answer we had to let ourselves in."

Without further ado, the convoy left the area just as lights started to illuminate the tower block. McCormick was unenthusiastic about the whole thing as it was pretty much a cosmetic exercise. Jim McCormick was a man who thrived on *real* policing, as he saw it, but withered under the weight of procedures and the mundane protocols. He glanced at Doyle who was studying the back of the seat in front but seemed otherwise at ease with his situation. McCormick knew Doyle was mentally preparing himself for two or three days of simply staring at something in the interrogation rooms of Castlereagh

Holding Centre. It might be a spec of something on the carpet, a stain on the table or a mark on the wall (or the wall itself). The interviewers would ask their questions and make their accusations, bully, browbeat, laugh, shout and whatever they felt it would take and Doyle and McBride would just sit there, staring at their chosen spot, letting it all wash over them. In the end, it would be the detectives who would give up and Doyle would be released without charge. McCormick sighed audibly at the thought of it.

"Are you bored, sir?" the overweight driver asked, glancing in the rear view mirror.

"Aye, but not for long," McCormick replied thoughtfully. "While the detectives and Doyle here strike up a meaningful relationship, I will be out and about bringing his mate Reilly in for a good tight grilling. He's the one I want. He's the one I have the goods on."

McCormick, of course, had no evidence against Reilly but it amused him to see Doyle flinch and glance quickly at him after he'd said it. That will get him thinking, McCormick thought to himself happily. He will wonder if what we have on Reilly will net him as well. Contented, McCormick closed his eyes and kept them shut for the duration of the journey.

When the prisoners were being processed in Castlereagh, McCormick decided to have a quick coffee in the canteen. He had had his day of fingerprinting and all that clerical rubbish. In the canteen he saw McCrum sipping a cup of something and reading a newspaper. It might seem very peculiar if I deliberately ignore him altogether, McCormick reasoned to himself. Decision made, he took his coffee over and sat opposite a startled McCrum.

"Act normally," McCormick hissed. "We don't want to make it too obvious that we don't have a working relationship." Then loudly, "Well, how's life in the fast lane, John? We brought you in new fish to fry. Doyle and McBride from Divis for the shooting yesterday. You might get a chance to meet them up close today!"

McCrum nodded thoughtfully. "Bad boys, are they?"

"Utter scum!" McCormick practically bellowed. "Even if they didn't try to shoot the two officers yesterday, they are guilty of something we have never caught them for, be sure of that! Lean on them, John. If nothing else we can give them a couple of hateful days. Don't be afraid to hint that we have an informant working close to them. Now don't be blatant about it but make it look as if there might be someone up there talking to us. That rattles the best of them!"

"Could you meet me in about half an hour and maybe give me a bit of background on them; a few pointers maybe?" McCrum asked plausibly.

"Certainly!" McCormick thundered. "I will teach you all I know about interrogations and everything there is to know about Doyle and McBride. After that, I must be off and find that degenerate Reilly. He will know by now that we hit his flat this morning so I will have to go a wee drive and see if he's out and about. You never know, John, I might just get lucky!"

A short time later McCormick and McCrum met supposedly to discuss the two suspects but in reality to share information and make arrangements for further contact later in the week. McCormick then left the holding centre and made his way to North Queen Street police station where he had a good working relationship with the Detective Inspector there. Before going there, he had browbeaten or persuaded Bryson to arrange for him to ride shotgun in a patrol or two in a bid to find Reilly or some word of him at least.

As they cruised the streets of north and west Belfast, McCormick watched studiously out of the passenger window in a bid to spot his quarry, the warrant for his arrest folded neatly in his jacket pocket, ready to be produced immediately. After just over an hour of driving through grids of streets, McCormick saw him! He was wearing a jacket with the hood up but there was enough of his face visible to ensure a positive identification. As they passed their quarry, McCormick radioed for the back up vehicles and then had the driver swing the car around to apprehend the elusive Reilly. The street was quiet so they were able to drive quickly towards him and cut in hard just in front of him. McCormick immediately jumped out of the car, gun in one hand and the warrant in the other, just as the back-up vehicles arrived. The driver shook his head as the adrenaline driven McCormick pointed his gun at the startled Reilly. "Unless Kojak!" the driver muttered.

Reilly did not put up any resistance. He was confident that he wouldn't be charged with anything and there was something about this cop, standing there pointing his gun like that. He was like someone who would be happy enough to pull the trigger and Reilly had no intention of giving him cause to do so. The officers in the back up vehicles seemed to fill the street as McCormick served the warrant, read Reilly his rights and left it to a uniformed officer to place the cuffs on the already extended wrists. The spectacle had attracted a few less than impressed bystanders who began to shout abuse at the police officers but McCormick was unmoved by it all. He had seen this kind of thing before and didn't seem at all bothered. As he lounged against the patrol car whilst the other officers contained the crowd and prepared to leave the area, he noticed something that struck him as strange. On the far side of the road, ignoring the melee, a man who looked to be in his early thirties, wearing a baseball hat and anorak, slouched past. There was something familiar about him and McCormick was immediately alert. He walked briskly towards the disinterested pedestrian ( a little *too* disinterested for McCormick's liking) and tapped him on the shoulder from behind. When the man turned around to face McCormick, the policeman *knew* he had seen him before.

"Do you mind telling me your name, sir?" McCormick asked politely.

"Jarlath Daly," the man replied.

"Jarlath Daly" McCormick repeated."Where are you from Jarlath?"

"Ballymurphy," Daly replied succinctly.

"Were you working away from home? You've lost your Belfast accent."

"Am I under arrest?" Daly countered. "It's just that I have to catch the train to Lisburn."

McCormick nodded and allowed him to continue on his journey but his interest was certainly aroused. That name was as fake as that accent, he thought as he walked back to the car. So who was that? McCormick grew irritated as he tried but failed to put a name to the face. With renewed determination, McCormick decided that he would identify the so-called Daly. Although he couldn't name him, he was fully aware of where he had known him from: Coleraine! And, if it was the same person he thought it was, he knew something else: 'Daly' was a Republican!

By the time he reached the car, McCormick had lost all interest in Reilly. He knew within minutes what he had to do and when he got to the station, he asked to see Bryson at his earliest convenience. His next item of business was to contact McNamee for a brief meeting that evening. The time and location was agreed and McCormick chuckled when he hung up as he considered the unmistakable reluctance in McNamee's voice. He then quickly scribbled a brief message on a piece of notepaper and, after a few furtive minutes of trying to make eye contact with McCrum, he walked towards his desk and let the note fall. It contained the time and location of the meeting with McNamee. McCrum was unsure what it was all about but committed the details to memory and then tore the note up.

When Bryson consented to see McCormick, the latter stood stiffly to attention before his boss.

"Take a seat, Jim", Bryson said irritated by McCormick's bearing. "What can I do for you?"

"Well, sir, I have been thinking. When John was killed in that bomb, you all thought I should have taken time off to get over it. Of course, me being me, I didn't listen. Well, I realise now that I *should* have listened and I *should* have taken time off. I am just not myself so, if the offer still stands, I would appreciate a few weeks to sort myself out and come back when I feel ready, really ready."

Bryson appeared amazed at this frank admission of

defeat from someone who was regarded far and near as an unstoppable force. He stared directly at McCormick who sat, legs crossed and his hands resting on his knees, the epitome of serenity.

"Well, if this was anyone else sitting there telling me this I wouldn't be surprised," Bryson began slowly, "but I have to say I am shocked to hear this coming from you, Jim. Of course our offer still stands. Take as much time as you need. I know you and Hargy were close and you are probably suffering from some kind of delayed reaction. Go to the doctor and see if he or she will give you something and don't worry about the latest arrests; we will have them thoroughly interrogated."

'I bet you will', McCormick thought as he stood to attention and thanked Bryson for being so understanding. 'It will be soft questioning and offers of cups of tea!'

That evening McCormick pulled up in the car park of the roadside cafe that had closed two hours earlier. He noticed that McCrum was already there and he congratulated himself on having asked his colleague to be there half an hour before McNamee. He parked beside McCrum and shouted for him to follow and then left the car park with McCrum tailing him. They parked on a side street in East Belfast and McCormick nodded for McCrum to leave his car and join him on the pavement. McCrum, as usual, silently obeyed and the two of them walked a short distance to a fairly old Volkswagen Polo. As they got into the car, McCormick offered a lesson in keeping safe.

"This is an old banger I picked up at an auction. When you're meeting the likes of McNamee, you can't afford to take any chances. He's a low life scumbag and a useless tout but you never know when he will sell us out. He might take a panic attack and tell his pals about our wee trysts and it could be them coming here this evening, not him, and if it's them, they will come packing. Never trust these touts, John. They are selling out their mates so they will sell out their enemies too if they have to. They don't know I have this car and after the recent lifts, they might be looking for a leak. We need to be careful at all times."

McCrum nodded, impressed at Jim's foresight. Admittedly he would never have thought about a precaution like this but, regardless of what he had heard about him, McCormick knew his job.

"Of course I had to buy this wreck out of my own pocket," McCormick continued. "The bosses are too busy buying Sinn Feiners dinners and fawning over the ones who are out there killing us to spend money on keeping us alive!"

They drove slowly past the deserted car park and, just as they were parallel with the cafe, McCrum noticed a car parked tight to the surrounding hedge. They swung around and parked tight to the car containing McNamee and McCormick nodded him out to join them.

"OK McNamee, this is John. Now I will be going away for a while so you will be meeting John from now on. Unfortunately for you, John is cut from the same cloth as me so don't expect a blind eye if you're up to any antics. And another thing, I won't be away forever so don't be giving John here the runaround while I'm gone or I will destroy you when I get back. You have my word on that, son!"

McNamee glowered and glanced at McCrum who stared back blankly at him. McCormick then gave McCrum a number of instructions and things he wanted information on from McNamee. The hapless informer sat as if playing the part of a one-man audience whilst the two cops spoke only to each other. Finally McCormick seemed to remember he was also in the car.

"Right,we're done here Joe so off you go," he said poetically. "But when John calls, you come running and no tricks or funny business. And if you hear *anything* about the bomb that killed John Hargy, you tell John straight away. It doesn't matter how trivial it might seem to you, tell John and *we* will decide how important the titbit is. Now off you go and get that Republic of yours sorted out. If you get up early enough in the morning, you might get to the Post Office in time to declare it before the women come in looking their family allowances."

When McNamee left the car, McCormick started the

engine of the Polo, leaving before his informer.

"Jim, you treat that fella like dirt," McCrum suggested. "How do you keep his loyalty? In fact, how come he even gives you any loyalty?"

"Lesson number whatever, John. You don't pander to scum like that. Treat 'em mean and keep 'em keen. Anyway, the likes of McNamee have no loyalties to anyone. No, he doesn't help me out of some sense of loyalty, John. He helps me because I am keeping him out of jail and I don't drop his name to any of his comrades. He also knows that if he stops helping me, I will do both."

McCrum nodded. "Can I ask where you're going?"

"Well, I would prefer that you didn't because I wouldn't be able to tell you and that might offend you. The thing is, John, say I were to tell you and then Bryson or his numb nut messenger boy Houston asks you, you have knowledge and you will have to lie to them. On the other hand, if you don't know anything, then you can safely and honestly say that without comeback. They won't be surprised as they don't know we are working together. So, the short answer is 'No you can't ask.'"

When they got back to their cars, McCormick bade McCrum the briefest of farewells and took off quickly, leaving McCrum wondering which direction his life was taking him. Sighing, he got into his car and drove home, keeping the radio off so he could think;

so he could piece everything together. By the time he got home, he was no nearer understanding any of it.

## Chapter 5

### *Another Dimension*

It was a bitter cold night and Declan McAleer believed he would never feel warm again. He had lit the fire in the squat living room hours ago yet he felt he might as well have lit a candle. The chimney was obviously in dire need of a good sweep but for now he would just add more peat turf and hope it would encourage heat instead of just thick smoke. Checking his watch, Declan noted that the others would soon be arriving at the derelict cottage so he fired up the ancient gas cooker and placed a similarly aged massive teapot on it, adding half a dozen teabags. He then took a seat on the sole chair and thought back on how he had gotten here.

Raised in the County Londonderry village of Swatragh, Declan was from a Republican family, steeped in that tradition. His maternal grandfather had bewitched him with tales of serving alongside Seamus Costello during the ill-fated 50s campaign. As he grew up, he heard even more exciting stories about his neighbours and people from the general area who had joined the IRA so that by the time he reached the age of eighteen, Declan McAleer couldn't wait to take the oath. However, he soon discovered that it wasn't like the films or second hand stories told to him by ageing relatives in the comfort of his living room. His first 'job' was to rob a rural Post Office with another young man from the area. The robbery had been a success of sorts in that it had been carried out without anyone getting caught but the two robbers had paid their visit to the Post Office too early; before the weekly intake of money had arrived so that when they were in a position to count the takings, they found they had only netted a few hundred pounds and a huge number of promotional bingo cards. Declan had been humiliated and derided but, due to his well placed family he had avoided being given a cruel nickname, unlike his co-robber who became known as "House" Malone.

After this, McAleer found himself carrying out tasks other than robberies. He had been uneasy about doing that one but had been persuaded that the money was needed to finance the war and to see to the needs of prisoners' families. Anyway, he had been told, the Post Office represented the British financial system locally so it was also a strike against them. When told he would no longer be involved in robberies, he took it as a rebuke but he soon got over it when he was asked to move an armalite machine gun from a hiding place (known as an arms dump) to behind a low stone wall one crisp frosty morning. He had carried out his duty to the letter and asked no questions. Later that day, he heard that an off duty UDR member had been shot and seriously injured at the point where McAleer had left the gun. He had been somewhat annoyed by this shooting and felt uncomfortable about his role in it. The reason he was upset was because he saw beyond the badge. The man who had been shot was known to McAleer; he was a mechanic who had often fixed his car and always for a fair price. He had always been kind and they shared many laughs at the injured man's garage. He approached his local commander and confided in him about how he felt and the effect the shooting had on him. The commander didn't hide his shock; this wasn't the reaction he expected from a volunteer! However, out of respect for the McAleer family, he decided to talk it all out with the young man. The commander argued that the mechanic had used his business to gather information on Republicans and his friendly manner had all been part of an act to win the confidences of locals so he could hear more information. McAleer agreed that this was possible and, encouraged by this, the commander continued. A mechanic, he said, was perfect cover for planting bugs and tracking devices. Had McAleer ever had his car checked? No, he admitted, it hadn't dawned on him. Again, this was entirely possible, he supposed. When the conversation ended, the Commander was satisfied that he had settled the nerves of the young volunteer and shown him the moral correctness of their cause. He hadn't seen this before but he had heard about it; a crisis of conscience that would either drive the bearer out of the movement or, if conquered, would never recur.

Even though the commander was content with the way the chat went, he decided that Declan would not play a pivotal role in the movement but would take care of peripheral things. Since then, McAleer was assigned low risk tasks like the one tonight; sourcing a safe place for a meeting where people could gather without interruption and without attracting attention. He had used this abandoned bungalow before because it was up a lane and was mostly hidden by an assortment of overgrown hedges and trees. The electricity had long since been disconnected but McAleer had rectified this by hooking up a generator. The isolation of the house meant that the noise emanating from the generator would not be heard and there was a rough yard that would hold at least three cars that could not be seen from the road. He hadn't been told the reason for the reason for the meeting or who would be attending it but that was standard form as the local commander was obsessive about his men only knowing what they needed to know. The appearance of headlights on the lane shook Declan out of his reminiscing and prompted him to go outside and see who had arrived.

First out of the car was the local commander who gave Declan a brief nod and went straight into the house. He was followed by the now named "House" Malone and Benny McGurran whom McAleer knew well. He followed them in to the smoky bungalow and apologised profusely to the others for the heavy smell of burning peat that seemed almost intoxicating. The commander was nonplussed by it all and waved a hand dismissively, congratulating McAleer for locating such a safe place to meet. The others nodded though they did wave their hands in front of their mouths as if to minimise the unavoidable smoke inhalation. The beams of another set of headlights distracted them all as a car made its way slowly up the lane. Declan went outside and directed the driver to a corner of the weedy yard and waited to guide the occupants indoors. He was surprised when the driver got out and turned out to be Hugh Maguire, a committed and frightening IRA man from outside Kilrea. Maguire was something of a legend and was said to have many good friends in the Belfast and Londonderry areas, leading Republicans his brother Joey had met and befriended when in prison for possession weapons and ammunition. According to the stories Declan had heard, the police had an informant close to Joey Maguire who played a key role in getting him arrested. The Maguire family visited him in prison and they discussed every aspect of the case and other incidents in the East Londonderry area like the discovery of arms and ammunition as well as an upsurge of arrests. The arrests hadn't led to any convictions but it was noted that on every occasion the police had lifted the right people. After much deliberation, the Maguires narrowed it down to one person who had known about the presence of the arms and would have known who had been involved in activities after the events. They were in fact correct in their assessment but felt it was pointless turning to the IRA for justice as they had obviously never suspected the man and might prove reluctant to deal with him. So, the Maguires resolved to settle the affair themselves and within a month, the informer was found drowned in the River Bann. Although it was deemed as suicide, it was widely known that the last person seen with the victim on the day of his disappearance was Hugh Maguire. He was interrogated by the police and the IRA but proved resilient to their questions and was subsequently released by both sets of captors. Since then, most people gave Hugh Maguire a wide berth or went out of their way to be of assistance to him regardless of what was asked of them.

McAleer didn't recognise the man with Maguire and whereas the latter grunted a 'Hello', the stranger walked straight past Declan without making eye contact. Declan followed them into the smoky living room and the commander told him to bring in cups of tea which he did, on a tray with a pint of milk but no sugar. The commander then instructed Declan to 'keep an eye on things out the front' before turning to the others. McAleer was stung by the dismissal and, as he stood outside shivering in the dark, he felt resentful. Whilst the others chatted in the house, he was sent outside to hang about alone. What was his contribution to whatever was happening indoors? To find and prepare an isolated place for a meeting, which he did. To try to make a fire and heat the place, haul a generator up that lane and provide electricity; which he did. To bring teabags and milk and serve tea like a maid; which he did. And then be sent packing when it came to the real business! Not only did he feel humiliated but it had been done in front of everyone! For as long as the meeting lasted,

McAleer's resentment grew.

Inside the cramped living room, the commander invited the stranger to address the meeting.

"Thanks for coming to meet me", he began, "my name is Josey McCloy and I have been sent down here to meet you all to discuss a wee problem we have. Without going into all the details, we have been using a volunteer from north Antrim for some very specific work. He has an expertise in explosives and has proved to be a very reliable and trustworthy volunteer. As you can imagine, the main theatre of the conflict is with us in Belfast and the security forces are watching our every move. Well, this fella comes to us when we have something special to do and he does it without fuss or failure. However, the other day he was heading for the train and he was stopped by the police; well not so much the police as one particular cop. He bluffed it off and the cop let him go but the chap is sure the cop recognised him. Now, we know a bit about this policeman. His name is Jim McCormick and for a few years he was based up in this are, or Coleraine to be exact. As part of North Region, he would have known our man as he lived just outside Ballycastle. McCormick shot one of our men dead a few years ago during a house search and he is one hard to sicken plod! He is like a dog with a bone and we reckon he will go after the explosives expert. You see, he made a bomb that killed McCormick's best mate. So, I am here to see what you can do to help me."

No one spoke for a minute or two and then the commander broke the silence.

"Well obviously we will do whatever we can, Josey. We would need to know where this volunteer lives and also where McCormick lives and details like that. Will you be needing some of our boys to go up to Belfast, do you think?"

Maguire interrupted immediately. "Count me out for that! No offence, Josey, but that place is riddled with touts. I would say that's likely why you need this boy to make your bombs and why you have come here to have that cop dealt with!"

McCloy shifted from one foot to the other uncomfortably as the commander grimaced visibly at this outburst. The others stared at the ground, intimidated by the presence of a Belfast man and afraid of Maguire.

"Well, I wouldn't put it like that, Hughie," McCloy began. "Certainly we have problems in that department and there's no point denying it but we aren't impotent. Like, we have plenty of men up there who are out operating. Do you really think we are fighting the war using just country folk? No, this volunteer is definitely the best bomb maker we ever seen and we want to protect him and who better to do that than his fellow country men. Look, there will be no need for any of you to go to Belfast. McCormick actually lives outside Antrim town, near

Aldergrove. Our man lives in Cushendall but he has moved into Coleraine since the incident with the cop. I can't tell you any more than that for now but we need you to draw up two sets of plans. One for an attack on McCormick's home and another for an attack on him when he visits his elderly mother at a nursing home in Antrim."

"OK," Maguire said quickly. "Addresses and details as soon as possible then, especially about the nursing home. It sounds like a place we could get away from in a hurry, straight to Toome where we can stay the night. Saves crossing the Bann where they will fire up roadblocks on every bridge."

McCloy promised to furnish Maguire with the details within a few days and left with him to travel out of the area to get his lift back to Belfast. McAleer watched them go and ventured back into the house. The commander nodded to him and left with Benny McGurran whilst "House" waited to get a lift home with McAleer. The pair of them extinguished the weak fire and loaded the generator into the back of McAleer's father's van. The friends said little to each other until Declan started the van. Neither of them noticed the hobbling silhouette leaving the darkened cottage behind them.

"Are you all right, Dec?" House asked with a degree of concern. "You're very quiet."

"I'm fine, House," McAleer replied weakly. "I suppose I know my place and it's obvious I am not trusted any more. Can't think why but tonight showed me that I am a skivvy and butler for the organisation so when you all have a meeting I know not to ask any questions. If they'd wanted me to know what was going on, they'd either have let me stay for the meeting or told me afterwards."

House looked genuinely surprised. "You got it all wrong, Dec! Like, you sorted out the whole meeting! If it wasn't for all your planning and organising, there wouldn't even have been a meeting! As if I would have known to have it in here and have a generator and all sorted out. And another thing, he could have picked any one of us to stand guard. Anyway get this van moving and *I* will tell you what happened in there. It was a load of talk anyway. I could have been snuggled up to Carol McDaid the night instead of sitting there half frozen and stinking with smoke with that psycho Maguire only a few feet from me!"

They both laughed and House told Declan what had transpired during the meeting as they drove along the dark winding road. When they parted company, House warned McAleer never to repeat what he had told him or even say that the conversation had taken place.

\*\*\*\*\*\*\*\*\*\*\*\*\*\*\*\*\*\*\*\*\*\*\*\*\*\*\*\*\*\*\*\*\*\*\*\*\*\*\*\*\*\*\*\*\*\*\*\*\*\*\*\*\*\*\*\*\*\*

Around the time Josey McCloy had left Belfast for his meeting near Swatragh, Jim McCormick was coming to the end of his hour long journey. Driving along a tree lined avenue in a middle class residential area of Coleraine, he scanned the houses looking for house numbers. It always infuriated McCormick that these people spent thousands on their homes yet so many of them kept their house numbers out of view. Of course, the house he was looking for wouldn't even have a house number on display but all he needed was for the house next door to have one and he would know where to go. He had been here before but only once and it had been a few years ago. Suddenly he saw a number on a white mail box and pulled in to the kerb. Leaving his old Polo, he walked briskly down the street, mentally counting the houses as he walked. After a short time, he reached his destination and walked directly to the front door, ringing the bell twice. Above him, a camera silently monitored him, a small red light flashing to the side. After a few minutes, the hall light came on and the solid front door opened cautiously.

"All right, Smithy! How's it going? Are you going to keep me standing here all night like a pauper?"

Detective Sergeant Martin Smith stood gaping at McCormick seemingly lost for words. When he had heard the door bell, he immediately flicked his television to the channel linked to the camera above the front door. He had stared at the image in disbelief because the figure at the door looked very like Jim McCormick who had been his boss a dozen years ago when he had transferred from an English force.

Thinking it couldn't be him, Smith had peeked through the curtain for a better look but his visitor was standing with his back to the window so he couldn't determine his identity. Lifting his personal weapon, he had another look through the small eye hole and, despite his disbelief, it looked even more like McCormick! When he opened the door, there was no mistaking it; it *was* McCormick!

"Jim!" Smith gasped. "What on earth are you doing here?"

"Still got that fancy English accent after all these years!" McCormick replied, deliberately ignoring the question. "It's Baltic out here, Smithy! At least make me a cup of coffee and give me a few minutes of your time!"

Smith stood aside and let McCormick pass by him into the hallway where he hesitated before seeing the comfortable living room through a dimly lit doorway. Before Smith could utter another word, McCormick fell back into the comfortable armchair nearest the open fire; Smith's favourite seat where he had been sitting before he went to answer the door.

"You have well for yourself, Smithy!" McCormick observed as he scanned the living room appraisingly. "me getting kicked back to Belfast done you no harm, it would seem. A wee bird told me you're a Detective Sergeant now. I'm impressed!"

Smith looked at his beaming visitor, still shocked to see Jim McCormick sitting in his living room.

"Well, maybe you moving back to Belfast helped me stay in the Force, Jim," Smith replied studying his old colleague. "You were a very irregular policeman with highly a irregular means of doing things. I have to say I wasn't always comfortable with your ….. ways."

McCormick laughed loudly. "My ways? Come on, Smithy, I got results! I never broke any laws, though maybe I bent a few, but at least the villains feared me. They knew if I was after them, the chances were they would be in jail within a very short space of time. Anyway, I taught *you* plenty, if I remember right. You came over here from England with all your fancy ideas but I like to think I kept you right."

Smith was amazed at McCormick's audacity. He had always been pompous and lived by a high moral code but here he was, taking credit for making him the policeman he was! Smith was about to protest but McCormick didn't give him a chance.

"Anyway, you know I was shipped out of here to protect someone. I was right about them killings back then and you know it too. When I saw that young fella who was killed in the car bomb leaving the house that night and followed the two strangers to Londonderry, I just *knew* they would wind up in Ebrington Barracks. That young fella – Brian something? - was being played by the spooks and look how it all ended! That Brian blown to pieces and the other two shot to bits outside Kilrea! Remember?"

Smith nodded gravely. "Yes, Jim, I remember. And I agree with you now as I did back then. Those young men were used and abused by the very people who were meant to be protecting this country and the people in it. It was a sordid business! And I have no doubt that it goes on today."

McCormick nodded eagerly. "You can be 100% sure it still goes on! And I let them know it too! I let them know that *I knew*! You were probably right to say less than I did but you knew too! But the top brass? Spineless bunch of pen pushers! They hadn't the guts to take on the Spooks and the politicians who sent them here to play their war games. Aye, I got shafted but what odds? I left this area with my head held high and haven't looked back! Until now, of course ....."

Smith stood up and walked to the curtained window, paused and then walked back, positioning himself in front of the cheery fire. He didn't know what was coming but he knew to dread it. McCormick had just landed here at his home out of the blue, without warning and without cause. He hadn't heard from McCormick in over two years and yet here he was, larger than life, sitting shooting the breeze as if calling in like this was something he normally did. Smith also pondered what McCormick had said and, more importantly, what he hadn't said. Taking the former first, McCormick had reminded Smith of the Loyalist killings that had taken place some years earlier. They had both been on the case, seeking to hunt down and imprison those responsible. As it transpired, one of the men involved in the killings had been compromised by Military Intelligence so their job was made that much harder. In the end, McCormick had followed the one who was compromised and that led him to a house used temporarily by Military Intelligence operatives. McCormick had followed the two undercover men that left the house after the Loyalist had departed and they had inadvertently taken him to Ebrington Barracks in Londonderry. This confirmed the role of the military and sent McCormick on a crusade to bring them all to account. He had failed when all but one of the Loyalists were killed, two shot dead by the army and the third blown to pieces in a car bomb which McCormick had been adamant had also been the work of the army. After the dust had settled, McCormick demanded answers and had been like a bull in a china shop. He had made enemies and plenty of them; politicians, senior police officers, the lot. In fact, he had made so many accusations and caused so much trouble that they had transferred him back to Belfast in a bid to silence him and rid themselves of the problem of Jim McCormick. Smith was well aware that McCormick had been absolutely correct in his estimation of what had occurred but he didn't agree with his methods of redressing the issue. He had refused to join McCormick in his noisy crusade and had implored his friend to use more subtlety but McCormick refused to listen. And now here he was, reminding Smith of all of that. But for what purpose?

"So what can I do for you, Jim?" Smith said smilingly, betraying his concerns.

"Well, Smithy, it's not a matter of what you can do for *me* exactly but more what you can do for *yourself*. I don't know if you heard but I had a good friend in the force up in Belfast who got blown to pieces a wee while ago. Not only was he a good friend; he was a first class cop! Anyway, he went to check out a bomb that had been left in a department store and it turned out that the one they found was a decoy. When he went to check out the rest of the place, the *real* bomb went off and blew him to pieces. A wife, young family left with nothing."

"I think I heard about that case," Smith replied, genuinely engaged. "Hargy was his name, wasn't it?"

McCormick nodded, looking mournfully into the fire. "Aye that was him. A bit like you and me back in the day, Smithy. We were different in every conceivable way yet we worked well together, complementing each other, I suppose. We were like that once, Smithy."

Smith knew emotional blackmail when he heard it yet no demands had been made. McCormick had yet to show his hand. So, playing safe, Smith simply nodded in understanding and agreement.

"Of course, the brass are the same everywhere and just as they turned on me up here, they have done the same in Belfast. I could accept being kept of the Hargy case because of how close we were but it's more than that! They have *excluded* me! I am persona non grata up there. You see, Smithy, the top brass are always working hand-in-glove with politicians. The Chief Constable and the ACCs aren't interested in law and order; they take their orders from politicians and civil servants. It's not about hunting down the bad guys and putting them behind bars where they belong. No,no,today it's all about checking with the politicians first to see if it's OK with them to hunt them down. We can't go annoying the poor terrorists nowadays because their political wing might be negotiating with our bosses and we can't upset the apple cart! So, they see me as a problem because I want justice for our dead colleague. They have kept me out of the loop and they would throw a party if I would just resign. Do you get the picture?"

Smith nodded. "Well, Jim, you were never going to get any prizes for subtlety and diplomacy. But I do sympathise with you. As you know, it's all very different up here. Yes we have had our shootings and occasional bombing but it's all contained. I have heard the rumours that the Provos are considering calling it a day and that we should adopt policing methods and make decisions with that in mind but I agree that that should *not* mean we should ease off in our pursuit of wrongdoers. In fact, it would be my opinion that we should squeeze them all the harder to bring the end sooner."

McCormick was impressed and encouraged. "Well said, Smithy, and I agree totally! I am delighted to hear this and, you know, I am not surprised! You were always a straight player and even though we made an odd pair, we thought the same way and I am delighted to learn that we still do! You see, I saw someone in Belfast, someone from up here. We were out lifting another scumbag for trying to kill a couple of our boys and I saw this character dandering down the street with his hood up. Well, naturally enough I went over and stopped him and asked him his name. Of course he gave me a false one; Jarlath Daly. He then tried to pass himself off as a Belfast man but his accent was as false as a Halloween mask and I *knew* that face! I couldn't place from where so I let him carry on but I would know him in a crowd, no doubt about that. He's from up here, Smithy, and he's working with the Provos up the road. My guess is he's the boy that made the bomb that Killed John Hargy!"

Although McCormick had stopped short of spelling out what he wanted, Smith at least now knew the reason for his visit: he needed help in identifying 'Jarlath Daly'.

"So how can I help, Jim? You need to be clear and speak in specifics, not riddles."

"I need a look at the family album, Smithy. I know for a fact that if I seen a mug shot of 'Daly', I would recognise him straight away. That's all I want; a name and, of course, an address and maybe car details and so on."

Smith considered the request. Normally a request such as this would be made through the proper channels, coming officially from a senior officer in Belfast to an equivalent rank in Coleraine. Then, he supposed, Jim McCormick wasn't a normal cop so why would he even consider following normal procedures? Also, he had a degree of sympathy for his old colleague. It was obvious that the senior ranks had turned their backs on him and not for any good reason. A quiet man by nature, Smith was a deep thinker. He saw the injustice of a policeman being prevented from doing his job and the further injustice of his bosses appeasing those who were still trying to kill them.

"OK, Jim, I will help you. Here's how we will do it. Tomorrow call the station and ask to make an appointment to see me. I will be free from 1.30pm until 3.00pm. We will meet in my office and I will have the photos there for you to look at undisturbed. If anyone asks, we are just a couple of old friends having a chat."

McCormick jumped to his feet and stretched out his hand. "I can't thank you enough, Martin! I owe you for this! And, just for the record, that's what we are- a couple of old mates having a yarn. The best of mates!"

With a minimum of further words, McCormick left his old colleague who watched him half running down the street towards his car. He shook his head as if in disbelief at McCormick's indomitable spirit and, as he closed the door, he was thankful for the Jim McCormicks of this world. They were needed too ….

Chapter 6

## *Who Said What?*

Although he was born Daniel Arthur Brennan, from childhood he was known as Dab, taken from his three initials. He had been lucky to survive childhood, being stricken by polio as a toddler mainly due to his parent's ignorance of inoculations and basic medical care. The Brennans were widely regarded as a harmless and inoffensive family who chose not to forge friendships outside of their household. They were seldom spoken about without evoking looks of pity and sorrowful shaking of the head. The father, Frank Brennan, was described as 'not quite right' and his wife Pat was regarded as a woman to be pitied, having a husband like that and all those children.

Daniel 'Dab' Brennan was the second of five children born to Frank and Pat and it was apparent early on that he had inherited his father's ways. The polio had left the young Dab with a pronounced limp but it was also evident that he had significant learning difficulties. Frank died of some illness when Dab was only seven years old and, as expected, the family refused to reveal what had taken Frank's life. The children went to the local primary school and showed remarkable ability given their home circumstances; all except Dab who only went to school occasionally and showed no compunction to learn anything and even seemed unable to undertake the simplest academic tasks. As the family grew, the children only left the family home to attend school, going directly home afterwards to study, except Dab, who would be seen wandering along the roads or across fields in a world of his own. Those who met him found that he was reluctant to speak to them or look them in the eye. Instead he tended to mumble incoherently whilst looking at the ground.

The other children eventually left home either to attend university or take jobs far from Swatragh and they were seldom seen again, aside from infrequent visits to see their ageing mother and increasingly eccentric brother. By the time he had entered his thirties, Dab had abandoned baths and all forms of social engagements but he did develop an ability to speak to people from outside his home, undoubtedly because the only one left there was his mother who was by then almost totally deaf. Even though Dab could have brief conversations with others, he preferred the company of the cows and sheep that grazed in the fields near his home he knew so well or the birds that soared above him and rested in the trees he loved to climb and sit in for hours. There wasn't a field, paddock, house or lane in a ten mile radius of Dab Brennan's home that he didn't know. He also seemed to know every fox hole, badger sett and rabbit hole in the same area. One thing he didn't seem to understand was the difference between day and night. Dab slept when he was tired and stayed in bed only while he slept. Neighbours would shake their head in wonder when, coming home from a night out, they would see Dab wandering along dark roads muttering away to himself. They would offer him a lift and he would refuse bluntly as was his wont. In the mornings, it was the same with workers heading off to their place of employment before dawn. They would see Dab in his 'uniform' of a padded black anorak, caked jeans and old boots limping along by roads or appearing out of lanes randomly, staring at them as they waved. No one had ever seen Dab Brennan in a car or eating food. He was just Dab the Danderer.

Although Dab had few talents, he had the power of thought. He could understand conversations and remember them though he found it difficult explaining what he had heard or seen. He did remember the other night, though. He remembered getting caught in that shower far from home and going into that wee empty cottage at the edge of the field he had been in. He found a snug corner of one of the rooms and settled down to wait for the rain to pass, covering himself with some old hessian bags for warmth. He couldn't remember when, but at some point he drifted off to sleep and remained that way until a noise awoke him. It was someone opening the door of the room he was in! He remembered lying perfectly still in the corner, hardly daring to breathe, never mind move. Whoever it was only came into the room a little bit, paused and then left, closing the door after them. Dab lay prone, wondering what to do before deciding to stay where he was. He hadn't seen the intruder but he heard whoever it was moving about in the next room. He heard the fire being raked of ashes, the grating metallic sound coming through the flimsy stud wall. The intruder then coughed and began to hum a tune that Dab didn't recognise (though he didn't recognise any tunes) so Dab knew it was a male. He didn't know how long had passed before he heard a car and more male voices. The voices were muffled when they were outside but they became clearer when they entered the next room. Then a second vehicle arrived and Dab heard doors closing and became very afraid. Now he couldn't go anywhere until they had all left! He hadn't intended listening to their conversation but he had heard every word they said. These were bad people and they were saying bad things. Dab didn't know Cormac but he knew that the people in the next room didn't like him and intended to harm him. It was a long time before Dab heard them leaving. First the two cars and then, after a little while, he heard muffled voices from outside and heard the rattle of a diesel van. After waiting another few moments, Dab got out from below the bags and went outside in time to see the van disappearing down the lane. He recognised that van: it belonged to young McAleer, the skinny one. Content that no one had seen him, Dab hobbled off into the night, deciding that it would be best for him to go home and stay there until the morning.

The next day, afternoon judging by the location of the sun, Dab was walking aimlessly along a narrow road, whipping tall weeds on the ditch with a thin stick. He had nowhere particular to go and was happy to pause at regular intervals to study the hedge growth and the field behind it. He was so lost in thought that he didn't hear the car coming along the road, nor did he notice that it was a police car. By the time he realised it was there, the car had stopped and the passenger window was going down.

"Well, Dab, how's it going?" the policeman said. Dab didn't respond but stared wide eyed at the policeman.

"What's wrong, Dab?" asked the driver, "You look like you've seen a ghost!"

Still he remained silent, staring terror stricken at the police car.

"I know you aren't much of a chatterbox, Dab, but you're worse than usual today. What's the matter? Is something wrong?"

Dab stepped forward and stared at the policemen, mouthing words silently.

"What is it? Are you in trouble?" the driver asked.

Dab shook his head. "Not me. Cormac. The bad boys will hurt Cormac!"

"Who's Cormac, Dab? One of your brothers?"

Dab shook his head and looked at the sky for a

moment before looking directly at the policeman.

"No! Cormac!" he said loudly. "Like you. Police!"

The policeman in the passenger seat got out of the car and offered Dab a bar of chocolate which he hesitantly accepted after rubbing the palms of his hands up and down his jeans in a bid to clean them. A conversation ensued which required much prompting and patience on the part of the policeman as he waited for Dab to answer each of his questions.

"Where did you hear this, about Cormac?" The answer came slowly. "Not today."

"Was it before it was last dark?" A nodding of the head in response.

"Can you remember who was talking about Cormac?" Pause. "The van. McAleer."

"Is this McAleer from around here?" Vigorous nodding.

"Has he many friends? Were his friends with him?" Slow nods. "Bad boys!"

"How do you know this, Dab? Were you with them?" Head moves rapidly from side to side.

"Then how do you know all this?" Pause. "I hear them talking in the room."

"What room was that, Dab? This is very important." Eyes widen. "The house!"

The driver left his seat and joined his colleague and Dab. "Will you show us the house, Dab? You aren't in trouble. We just need to know."

Dab nods and points vaguely in the direction of Swatragh. Without another word he starts walking, beckoning them to follow him. The two policemen got into the car and took off in the opposite direction, looking for a place to execute a three-point turn. "This could be a wild goose chase," the driver driver observed, turning the car.

"I know," replied his passenger, "but even though I haven't a clue what he's on about, he knows *something*. Have you any idea who this Cormac might be?"

The driver shook his head and sighed. If nothing else this will kill some time, he reasoned. Up ahead, they lost sight of Dab so the driver accelerated the car. As they passed the end of an overgrown lane, the passenger caught sight of Dab hobbling up the narrow track and the driver braked and reversed back a few feet.

"What do you think?" the passenger asked.

"I don't like it," replied the driver. "Let's wait and see if he comes out. Although I'm not sure what he was on about, there could be danger up there. I will drive up the road and turn and see if we can catch up on him and see what this is all about."

The two cops sat in their car and waited but Dab didn't return to the road. After about fifteen minutes, they decided to head back to the police station as to sit about any longer would only get them noticed. When they got back to the station, they immediately told the sergeant about the conversation with Dab and he advised them not to go back to the house but to give him the details of the location of the house, including the coordinates. The sergeant then assigned them to other duties and the two colleagues set off to complete the fresh tasks. As soon as they left, the sergeant placed a call to his superior.

The next morning, Detective Sergeant Martin Smith sat in the best furnished and most comfortable room of the police station surrounded by his colleagues for their weekly conference. He hated these meetings where the senior ranks took the main stage to congratulate themselves and offer undue criticisms of others. Smith tapped his pen absent-mindedly on the blank pad before him and waited until the great and the good were ready to offer their pearls of wisdom. He was surprised, though, to notice the presence of some CID people he knew and two others whom he guessed were Special Branch. This was highly unusual as these meetings were normally about routine policing matters within the divisional command area and not normally a place for Special Branch. Smith noticed that most of his colleagues were casting the two strangers furtive glances but the objects of their curiosity seemed not to notice or were content to ignore the uneasy looks. A sharp series of taps on the he desk from the pen of the Divisional Commander indicated that the meeting was about to begin.

As expected, the first half hour was taken up with mundane issues and only a very few made an effort to appear interested. Then an Inspector spoke on a matter that commanded Smith's full attention. The inspector then began to inform the meeting about a report that had received from CID based in Coleraine. He then offered his assembled colleagues a paraphrased account of the intelligence report and Smith couldn't help but notice the smirks and rolling eyes of most of the others as the Inspector told of clandestine meetings of 'bad boys' held in a derelict house somewhere near Swatragh and the source being a local slow-witted loner whom even the local police regarded as a misfit. However, as the inspector drew his narrative to a close, Smith suddenly took interest in the discourse; when the inspector mentioned 'Cormac'.

"Do we know where this house is?" he enquired, not failing to notice that 'Cormac' sounded remarkably like McCormick and, if the source had learning difficulties then it may well be Jim the 'bad boys' had been discussing.

Before the Inspector had a chance to respond, one of the Special Branch men quickly spoke up.

"Yes we know the location of the house and it is now under our jurisdiction and we are taking charge of the surveillance and entire investigation," he blurted out before adding, as if an afterthought, "with the consent of the Divisional Commander, of course!"

Smith looked from the speaker to the Inspector who simply nodded. McCormick would hate this, smith pondered. They really are a law onto themselves with their cheap suits and bad ties!

"Well, have we any idea of the identity of 'Cormac' at least?" Smith pressed.

The inspector seemed to recoil a little and outstretched his arm to the Special Branch man who seemed to give the matter some thought before replying.

"There are a number of people it could be. The difficulty lies in the ability of the source or, rather, his inability to discern things. We realise that this could be a wild goose chase but there are a lot of 'bad boys' in that area so we are going to pursue this. The whole area is currently under scrutiny and we need to keep routine patrols to a bare minimum. If there *are* meetings taking place at that house, we want to see who attends."

The meeting broke up and Smith immediately left to collect the mugshots for his meeting with McCormick. Could it be Jim they are targetting, he wondered. But why? Why would the IRA in the Swatragh area be interested in a Belfast-based cop who lived near Antrim? Unless all of this has something to do with 'Jarlath Daly'.......

Within the hour, Smith's door knocked sharply and, without invitation, McCormick strode into the office and gave the room an appraising look.

"Well, now Smithy!" he began, smilingly, "This is some spot you have here! Photos of the wife, a nice pot plant and a room with a view! More like a hotel than a cop shop! You *have* done well for yourself! Remember the dungeon I had in the old barracks? Had to burn the light all day long it was so dark in it, even in summer!"

"Yes, it's very nice but a nice office doesn't solve crimes, Jim. You did very well in your cave! Anyway, here we are; the photo album from Hell. Take your time and look at each one carefully."

"I'm not a middle aged wife who got mugged on her way to the shops, Smithy," McCormick said huffily. "I only need to see a glimpse of him to know if he's 'Daly'. And if he isn't in your collection, I will know in five minutes, believe me!"

Smith shuffled some papers as McCormick went

through the photographs. Although they hadn't worked together for a long time, Smith was acutely aware of McCormick's enormous belief in himself and his off-hand manner. Best let him get on with it, he mused, as he began to read a memo about traffic issues in and around Garvagh.

Suddenly the silence of the office was shattered by McCormick who stabbed a particular photo with his forefinger and exclaimed loudly, "That's him! That's Daly! Who is he?" he asked leaping from the chair.

"Are you sure, Jim?" Smith asked, recovering from the shock of the shouting. McCormick glared back with his eyebrows raised and Smith offered him his open hands by way of apology for ever doubting his excited colleague. He then looked up the corresponding file.

"His name is Sean McDermott and he has a number of addresses from Cushendall to Ballycastle. It says here he is an electrician by trade and, yes, he is a suspected bomb maker but little more is known about him."

"That's him!" McCormick repeated loudly. "I know something about him; he murdered John Hargy! They brought him to Belfast for that job and maybe others for all I know! I must get McCrum to check the make-up of that bomb and see if it matches any others. Then I will shake down some of them wee touts up there and see if 'Daly' was about when they went off. Smithy, he was taking the train back when

I stopped him. I wonder is there a surveillance camera at the station he boarded? Let me see, from either Cushendall or Ballycastle, if he took the train, he would have got on it at either here in Coleraine, Ballymoney, Cullybackey or Ballymena. I don't think there's even a ticket seller at Cullybackey so we will have to hope he got on either side of it. Has Ballymoney a camera though?"

"Jim, let's go for a coffee," Smith said quietly. "There are a few things we need to talk about."

When they had been served by a busy waitress in a small cafe with ample condensation on the window glass, Smith told McCormick all about the briefing that morning. As was his wont, McCormick interrupted as he saw fit and then sat quietly for a few minutes after Smith had finished his account.

"You think 'Cormac' is me?" McCormick asked, already knowing the answer. Smith nodded.

"Let's look at the whole picture, Jim, and fill in a few of the blanks. John Hargy is killed in a bomb and shortly after that, you stop someone you think you recognise and he gives you a false name. Then a local yokel hears about someone he calls 'Cormac' who is in danger from 'bad boys', presumably the IRA, given the location of the meeting. My guess is that our friend 'Daly' AKA McDermott has been spooked because he also recognised *you* and went crying to the Provos up here and they have decided to take you out, my friend."

McCormick nodded in agreement. "Or McDermott went crying to Belfast and they have sent word down here for them to clip me." Smith nodded and shrugged his shoulders. "Does it really matter where the order came from?" he asked.

"It matters, all right!" McCormick retorted. "If it came from Belfast then our friend McDermott is someone special and they have more work for him to do. This isn't some tribal thing where the ones up here are trying to protect their own; it's the Big Chiefs looking to protect their golden boy. We have to get him, Smithy! If they need him enough to kill me then we need to take him out of circulation!"

"We need to be careful here, Jim," Smith began cautiously. "Special Branch are in control here and I know you can't stand them but they're calling the shots here and if you meddle, you'll have no cover. The bosses will hang you out to dry and the Provos will kill you anyway. Will you go easy at least? Like, work with me here?"

"OK, we will play it your way," McCormick responded. "And before you think I have gone soft, let me explain why. The Branch don't know bout my run in with McDermott. They don't know he murdered Hargy. So that really isn't anything to do with this meeting in the house they are so precious about. In other words, we can do our police work on McDermott without linking him to this meeting. That way we can do what we need to do and we aren't interfering with the cheap wardrobes!"

Smith couldn't disagree with McCormick's logic. The two parted company to do their respective things. Operation McDermott had, quite unofficially, begun.

As soon as McCormick returned to his hotel, he rang McCrum and instructed him to call him later that evening between 6.30pm and 7pm. He then pored himself a strong cup of coffee and thought about everything he had discovered. The more he thought about it, the more he believed that the whole web was spun around McDermott and that that chance encounter he had with him when he passed himself off as 'Jarlath Daly' was the reason his life was now in grave peril. Well, he decided after a lengthy period of contemplation, we will see who gets caught in this web! McCormick naturally decided that it wouldn't be him.

His pacing, mumbling and thought process was suddenly interrupted by the phone ringing. He snatched the receiver and found McCrum on the other end.

"I need a favour," McCormick said instead of the customary 'hello' but McCrum had learned to ignore his friend's abandonment of pleasantries if he was preoccupied with weightier matters. Without waiting for McCrum to reply, McCormick forged ahead. "I need you to meet that half-wit McNamee. The scumbag who killed Hargy is now looking my scalp as well because I spotted and stopped him. He doesn't know yet that I know his real identity and that's how I want to keep it. So, when you get a hold of McNamee ask him about an outa town bomber called Daly or McDermott. My thinking is that if he used 'Jarlath Daly' when I stopped him, he might just be known as that among the rank and file of the Provos up there. OK?"

McCrum nodded absent-mindedly before realising that McCormick couldn't see that nod so answered with a brief, "OK, got it. I will be in touch as soon as possible. I will see McDermott tonight and get back to you as soon as I can."

McCormick hung up quickly and left his hotel for a drive around his old stomping ground. He drove first to Ballymoney and then made for the nearby village of Rasharkin. As he drove up the main road to the village, he decided, spontaneously he believed but in reality it had been his sub conscious intention all along, to take a right a few miles short of Rasharkin in the direction of Kilrea. In less than ten minutes he was crossing the River Bann within sight of the town. He decided to drive slowly through Kilrea, looking around him without knowing what he was actually looking for or who. Although Smith hadn't told him the exact location of the house under scrutiny, he had given him the general whereabouts and, despite himself, McCormick just *had* to see it. He acknowledged even to himself that it was pointless and maybe even foolish and definitely pointless, yet he had to do it. As always, McCormick quickly found himself capable of justifying his actions. They were planning to KILL me, he thundered to no one. I have a right to see where my murder was planned! Heading along the road from Kilrea towards Upperlands, he kept an eye out for the road that would lead to Swatragh, narrowly missing a wandering odd looking fellow who seemed oblivious to everything around him. The fool was walking along at least two feet from the ditch and failed to notice that McCormick had to swerve violently to avoid knocking him down! McCormick glared into the rear view mirror and watched the ambling local continue on his journey as dusk fell, seemingly unaware that he had almost been killed. Muttering angrily to himself, McCormick almost missed the entrance to the lane but, at the last minute he saw it. He drove up a little bit further and parked up, stepping out of his car to have a look over the hedge. He saw the cottage and the crumbling buildings around it but couldn't see any electrical cables leading into it. He stood another minute or two before jumping back into the car and driving off towards Coleraine. A rats nest, he thought angrily. And rats planning their mayhem within it!

Around the time McCormick left his hotel that evening, a team of engineers, under orders from Special Branch, made their way quietly and stealthily along a thick hedge to the back of the cottage. They had entered a field from a narrow road, seldom used apart from local farmers, and walked bent over along the hedge, their camouflage blending in with their surroundings. Their orders were the normal kind for an operation like this. Enter secretly, disturb nothing, plant the listening devices and leave unobserved. It would be an operation best done at night but there could be another meeting of whoever they were spying on so it had to be with a certain element of risk and at dusk. When they entered the cottage, the smell of charred wood and peat ash from the fire mixed with the stench of rot and decay was pungent. It looked like the meetings were held in just one room, the living room. The other two rooms looked unused though the stinking kitchen suggested signs of use with markings on a dusty table indicating what looked like marks left by cups and possibly a kettle. The team worked quickly yet carefully, placing the bugs in various locations throughout the living room and kitchen with a couple in the cluttered room beside the living room. Their job done, they left as quietly as they arrived, unobserved by anyone as they walked back along the same hedge in the gloom of early evening.

Smith was surprised to receive a summons to meet the Divisional Commander at eight the following morning. He immediately felt a nervousness he hadn't experienced in years. This was the first time ever the Commander had asked to see him; not that he had *asked.* It had been a short clear-cut command and that hadn't brought him any comfort. His wife suggested that it might be something positive like a promotion or a commendation but Smith was unconvinced. A pessimist by nature, he had a deep sense of foreboding about this particular meeting. So, at 7.50am the next morning, Smith sat nervously in an uncomfortable seat in a shiny corridor outside the room commissioned by the Divisional Commander for the meeting. Five minutes later he was called inside.

"Take a seat,Detective Sergeant," the Divisional Commander ordered, pointing to a chair in front of his desk. He then carried on reading some papers as Smith sat waiting with an even greater sense of anxiety. Finally his superior office laid the papers on the desk and stared at the uneasy Smith.

"I have asked to see you this morning in the hope that you can help me clear up something of a mystery," he began pleasantly enough. "I have here a report from our colleagues in Special Branch which I received last night. The content shocked me so much that I actually met with the Officer in Charge to see if the report is factual, such is the content of it."

He paused and looked at Smith sternly, his countenance changing from one of pleasant openness to one of open hostility. Smith shifted slightly in his seat.

"As you are fully aware, the house where we believe the IRA has used for a meeting place is under surveillance and out of bounds to all but SB and their specialist units. Well, yesterday evening, a car pulled up along the roadside and the driver got out and looked across the fields in the direction of the house.

The driver wasn't identified but the owner of the car was, and the person seen yesterday fits the description of the registered owner of the car. Now, would you like to hazard a guess as to whom that might be, Smith?"

Although Smith immediately and instinctively knew, he couldn't bring himself to believe it.

"No, sir", he said, his face as blank as he could make it. "I have no idea."

"Really, Smith? McCormick! Yes, no less a man than Jim McCormick! Now what would he be doing peering into a house where, we believe, a meeting to discuss his murder took place! And as McCormick is supposed to be safely ensconced in Belfast, what or *who* would bring him down here? It wouldn't take Sherlock Holmes to see that he couldn't have known about that house unless someone told him about it! Well, I took the opportunity to call his superior officer, John Greer, and what did I discover? Jim McCormick is off on sick leave after the murder of his colleague, John Hargy. So what can I concur from this? Well, obviously big Jim decided to spend his sick leave in the countryside in the hope of fresh air will hasten his recovery. How am I doing, Smith?"

If Smith had had McCormick in front of him at that moment, he would have knocked him out cold. What was Jim thinking of? Was he even thinking at all?

"Well, sir,I don't know what to say. Jim *was* in touch

with me but about another matter altogether. It actually concerned someone who came from here but has been seen in and around Belfast. A Republican as it happens. Nothing whatsoever to do with the alleged meeting of locals." Smith looked straight at his superior hoping that his manipulation of the facts had seemed plausible enough to fool the Commander.

"And who exactly was this Republican, Smith?"

"I can't recall as it was a brief conversation but I believe his name was Daly. I brought Jim into my office and he looked at a few mugshots but he didn't see this Daly amongst them. Sadly I wasn't able to help him so he left and I haven't seen him since."

"So there was no cosy chat about developments here?" The Divisional Commander asked.eye brows raised.

"No, sir," Smith replied convincingly, "but you must bear in mind that Jim was stationed here for quite some time and knew quite a few officers. He was a well respected officer amongst the rank and file at least. Maybe someone he knew from his time here spoke to him about the house. I know it was meant to be confidential but we can't account for canteen talk."

The Divisional Commander paused and gazed out of the window.

"Yes, Jim was a popular officer and his heart is in the right place but he had a real problem with authority. He was too headstrong and a maverick with no appreciation of politics and he stubbornly refused to accept that there are other agencies at work here and we sometimes have to work with them!" Turning to Smith he continued. " McCormick wasn't beyond having informers working for him, you know? He had an incredible knack of bending the rules without breaking them. My advice is, if he contacts you again, keep your distance. And tell him nothing! You can go, Smith."

Dismissed like a naughty schoolboy, Smith went to his office and held his head in his hands. He could cheerfully kill McCormick yet he knew he wouldn't. He knew he would help him. That was just the way it was and not only did Smith know it but McCormick knew it too.

# Chapter 7

## *A Tangled Web*

It had been a long time since McCormick had been to this particular house but he was confident that the man who occupied it on his last visit would still be the occupant. Like a coyote, this specimen never travelled to far from what he knew. He parked a few doors away from the house and walked down the street, keeping his eyes peeled before knocking loudly on the front door. The hall light came on and the door opened, basking McCormick in light.

"Long time, Harry!" McCormick announced as a bewildered and aged Harry Bradshaw stared back in disbelief.

"McCormick!" Bradshaw uttered, blinking hard as if unable to believe his eyes. "I don't know where you came from but you can go straight back there!" He started to close the door but McCormick shot his hand out and pushed the door wide open and brushed past Bradshaw into the kitchen.

"See! I still remember the layout of your house! Isn't that impressive? Anyway, enough about me. How are you, Harry? You look like you're a hundred years old! Are you sick?"

Bradshaw slowly walked into the kitchen and sat down heavily on a soft chair by the window and continued to stare at McCormick as if it was all a bad dream.

"Sick?" he replied eventually,"I am sick and tired of the life I live! I sit here every day waiting for night to come just to get the day done. You know why? Because of you, McCormick! I rue the day I ever agreed to work with you! I should have let you book me for drink driving all them years ago and took the consequences. Another few years inside would have been nothing compared to what I lost by getting mixed up with you!"

McCormick smiled cheerfully. "Aw come on, Harry, we had our moments. I actually thought we had become good friends at one point. Anyway, my old son, I didn't tell you to get full drunk and try to drive a car from Londonderry to Coleraine with a prison licence hanging over you. You made that decision all by yourself, mate. And you could have refused my offer, you know? It wasn't mandatory, you working for me, giving me the odd titbit. No, Harry all of the problems you've had are down to decisions *you* made. I was just a spectator."

"Because of you I lost my nephew!" Harry shouted back. "Alec was the only relative I had who believed in me. After his mates were shot dead and the other one was blown to pieces, he blamed me! He left for England after that and I haven't heard from him since and likely never will! He sees me as nothing but a tout!"

"But you *are* a tout, Harry!" McCormick replied grinning. "OK, you were never much of an asset but you served your purpose. I bet you that when I was shipped back to Belfast no other cop showed you the understanding I did. I suppose that was you off the hook, right enough, me departing for the Big Smoke. I never told any of the others about you, you know? Nope, you were my special wee buddy. So, where's the wife?"

"Gone!" Bradshaw snarled. "She's gone, my old comrades have their suspicions about me and my family ignore me. You have no idea how much I hate you, McCormick!"

"No, Harry, you hate yourself but if pretending that it's me you despise helps, I don't mind. Anyway, do me a favour and cast your mind back to the good old days. Did your boys ever mention a Provo called Sean McDermott from Ballycastle or the Glens area?"

"You have some neck on you asking a favour from me!" Harry retorted. "I can't remember anything about anyone."

McCormick nodded and made for the kitchen door. "Give me a name, Harry. Give me someone worth approaching, for old time's sake. One of your old side kicks."

Bradshaw gazed at the floor and didn't respond.

"I understand, Harry," McCormick said as he walked towards the front door. "You can't cope with good byes. I'll let myself out."

As he walked to his car McCormick tried to get all of his thoughts in order. He had drawn a blank with Bradshaw and wouldn't be visiting him again. The man was beat; beaten by the life he had chosen and now that he was no good to anyone, everyone had deserted him. McCormick shrugged. He brought it all on his own head. He jumped in the Polo and headed back to the hotel.

The receptionist was always pleasant and seemed genuinely happy to see McCormick as he strode into the lobby.

"Mr McCormick, I have three messages for you from the same number and the caller asked if you could call him back as soon as possible," she gushed as if she had practised that sentence and was reciting it from memory.

In his room, McCormick read the number aloud as he punched in the digits. A local number, he mused as the ring tone began.

"That you, Jim?" asked Smith on picking up the receiver. When McCormick had confirmed it, Smith told him to be in the car park of a nearby shopping centre in 30 minutes outside a specific shop. The line went dead and McCormick wondered about the terse voice and abruptness of his old friend.

When McCormick arrived at the car park, Smith was already there and quickly joined his former boss in the Polo.

"I actually have no idea what on earth possessed you to go to that house, Jim!" Smith exploded. "I was pulled in about it by the Divisional Commander and they know it was you as they got your car registration!" Smith then repeated the conversation he had had with the Chief and then paused for a response.

"Well, you seem to have covered it rightly, Smithy," McCormick replied happily. "OK, I know it was stupid but I was just interested, I suppose. A human failing and it won't happen again. Have you anything else for me? Aside from the fact that the house is obviously under surveillance and therefore most likely bugged."

Smith shook his head and then made an excuse that he had another place to go without saying where. They parted company and McCormick returned to his hotel for the evening to think over all the information he had gleaned. It could be a long night, he mused. A pity Greer now knows where I am. I better avoid phoning the office for a day or two ……..

On the day the specialist team were busily planting bugs in the derelict house, Declan McAleer had a delivery to make first thing that morning. As he was running late, he threw the bags of cement into the back of his van hurriedly and set off as fast as his old van would go. As he drove along the narrow country roads, his mind was on the job as he tried to calculate if he had indeed loaded enough cement for the bricklayers to make a start on the house they were building. He tried to recall his conversation with them the previous day and couldn't remember if they had said ten or twelve bags. He had loaded on ten and decided that if more were needed, he could always go back for the remainder. His father had been the small business some years before and was now supplying building contractors and independent bricklayers across counties Londonderry and Antrim. Declan had only recently joined the business, working four days a week with plans to do his own thing before much longer.

The parked car was almost in front of him before he saw it as he turned a mild corner. He didn't have time to think about what to do but tried to go out around it whilst simultaneously braking hard. He felt the van glide across the road in a skid and didn't think to take his foot off the brake. The last thing he could remember seeing was a huge tree he was approaching at speed and then he heard the horrendous smash as the van struck it broadside.

And then there was nothing.

When Declan regained consciousness he was in a hospital bed but the diagnosis was good. Aside from some bruising and a knock to the head, no bones had been broken and he would although he was being kept in overnight, he would be discharged in the morning. He spent the day convincing concerned relatives that he was fine and they had nothing to worry about although he was suffering from a thumping head ache and in the late afternoon he slipped into a deep sleep. When a nurse gently woke him, he was disorientated and it took him a few minutes to remember what had happened and where he was but, as his bleary eyes cleared, he saw two uniformed policemen. The interview didn't last long and the police assured Declan that the owner of the parked car was at fault and that they would file a report to support this for insurance purposes. When they left, Declan drifted back to sleep, his headache abated.

---

That night the derelict house played host to another clandestine meeting. Under the cover of darkness, two vehicles made their way up the rough, overgrown lane a few minutes apart. Out of the first car stepped the local IRA commander, House Malone and Benny McGurran. They went into the darkened house to await Hugh Maguire.

"Trust Declan to roll the van!" the Commander grumbled. "This place is freezing and I can't see a thing! He would have had the lamps lit and a fire on if nothing else."

"Aye," House agreed. "He has lit many a fire for Ireland, our Declan!"

They all laughed and then the Commander pointed out that everyone had a role to play and that although Declan's given role was not pivotal, it had importance. Anyway, he argued, was it not better that he should be given something to do that he was capable of instead of something he couldn't do? That could spell danger to them all. Just then they spotted the dimmed headlights of a car coming into the yard. Maguire had arrived.

"Right, boys?" he asked briskly. "Where's the other one? The skivvy?"

The Commander explained about the accident and Maguire seemed satisfied.

"We have had a loot at McCormick's house and there hasn't been much activity. We think he's there because his car is in the garage and the lights are on for a while in the house at night. Now, the ones watching the house haven't actually seen him but they aren't there all the time so they might miss seeing him. Anyway, we have it in good authority that he's not well and has taken time off work. There's no obvious surveillance on the house from the police and my view is that we should hit it tomorrow night."

"It's a bit short notice, Hugh," the Commander objected. "We won't be able to pull it together that quickly. Is it *that* urgent?"

"Two things," Maguire replied. "Belfast wants this sorted as soon as possible and I don't want us looking incapable of doing this. Secondly, I have the planning done with the boys up there. I will take the shooters up tomorrow afternoon to the safe house. The weapons will be there and the boys from Crumlin are supplying a car and a driver. All we need to do is provide two men for the job. Well, you two?"

House and Benny looked at the Commander and he nodded. They then turned their gazes to Maguire and nodded their agreement.

"No problem, Hugh," House said awestruck at the opportunity to do a favour for the notorious Maguire.

"OK. Pack old clothes into a bag and I will meet you at Donnelly's tomorrow at 5 o'clock in the afternoon. You will be staying away tomorrow night so make an excuse to you own ones. We don't need worried mothers reporting you missing to the police."

Without further ado, the meeting ended and they parted company. The Commander warned them to be careful and be sure to tell their folks that they wouldn't be home the following night. He was the man in charge but he was also wary of Maguire and didn't want his boys letting him down.

---

The door of McCormick's hotel room shook with the ferocity of the banging and Jim wasn't sure what to do. He demanded to know who it was and was relieved when Smith replied that it was him.

"Jim, I have some news for you," he said as he rushed into the room. "The boss has told me there was a meeting in the derelict house last night, a short but important meeting. To cut to the chase, they are coming for you tonight. They believe you are at home because apparently your car is in the garage and your lights come on in the evening. The hit team will be two men from either Kilrea or Swatragh. We can't say for certain as no names were mentioned at the meeting except a 'Declan' who wasn't present. And your name, of course."

For a few moments McCormick said nothing but stared in a startled fashion at Smith. Then he regained his composure.

"Who's in charge of the case? What do you think I should do? Have you no idea who is doing the shooting?"

"Easy, Jim!" Smith said sternly. "There is no 'case' as such but the investigation is under the control of Special Branch and their 'friends'. I think you should phone Greer who is frantically trying to locate you and when you *do* phone him, in my presence, you will sound calm and collected and assure him that you are up here for respite and you will do as the Divisional Commander here says *and* that you will not interfere in any way. Finally, I honestly don't know who the death squad is composed of but the surveillance team identified two cars, one belonging to the local IRA commander, Jim Bryce, containing several people and the other owned by and, we believe, driven by Hugh Maguire from Kilrea."

"OK,Smithy! I think I will put myself under your protection and come with you to the station. No doubt you will be privy to what's going on so at least I will be informed of my murder, as it were. Good job I bought them timer gadgets that switches lights on automatically. I only bought them to deter thieves but there you have it! Right, time to call Greer and tell him his Republican mates won't get me tonight! Hope he doesn't tip them off!"

Smith rolled his eyes and nodded to the phone and waited as McCormick convincingly assured his boss that he was well and would be 'stuck to Smith like glue' until it was all over. Then the pair travelled to the police station in Coleraine with Smith wondering should he lock McCormick in a cell for all their sakes.

---

Maguire seemed to check his watch every two minutes as he waited for the driver to arrive at the safe house. House Malone and Benny McGurran watched him quietly, not wanting to seem nervous or irritate him with small talk. From the time he had collected them earlier, he had gone from talking incessantly to prolonged silences without explaining his deep thoughts. Repeatedly he had told them the fairly straightforward plan. The driver would take them to the house, Malone would have a sledgehammer to smash in the front door and as soon as it was in, McGurran would enter first. Malone would then discard the sledgehammer and quickly follow and he would take the downstairs while McGurran sought their prey upstairs. As soon as the job was done, they would get back into the car and be taken to the safe house. The boiler suits and gloves they were wearing would be taken off enroute left in the car to be burned by the driver. They would have baths in the safe house to get rid of any residue and then dress in the clothes they brought with them. Next day they would be taken home and the job would be done. Maguire was at pains to reassure them how grateful 'Belfast' would be. He conceded that shooting a policeman at his home was not an ideal plan but there was an urgency to this hit and they had to strike him where they could get him so at his home it was then.

At 9.50pm, the car arrived and Maguire wished them 'Good luck' as they left in their boiler suits and gloves, their balaclavas rolled up like hats on the top of their heads. The driver indicated that the sledgehammer was on the floor of the back seat and the guns were beside it. The two assassins quickly found them and checked the guns with House Malone laying the sledge hammer across his knees in readiness. The journey lasted less than five minutes and the driver pulled up at the front door and, as the gun men got out, the driver set about tuning the car for a quick getaway.

The front door of McCormick's house gave way on the third attempt and McGurran pushed it open as splinters cracked and snapped around him. He ran down the hallway and went straight up the stairs his gun ready. Malone quickly discarded the sledge hammer and went straight to the living room. It was empty but the television was on (switched on by an undercover team from E4a who had entered the house early that morning before sunrise). Suddenly he heard a shout or scream (with the balaclava fully pulled down, it was hard to tell which) followed by a succession of four gunshots. Benny has got him! Malone thought to himself with elation. He turned around and ran to the bottom of the stairs to await his friend coming down but what he saw terrified him. Benny McGurran lay at the top of the stairs, his torso on the small landing, his head and shoulders hanging from the top step, blood streaming through the balaclava and matter pouring from the eye holes. For a moment Malone was too shocked to move, his eyes fixed on his dead friend in morbid fascination. Then he came to his senses and turned swiftly to run out of the shattered door. The last thing he saw was a shadowy figure standing a few feet from him, a gun pointed directly at him. Before he could utter a sound, he felt the force of the bullets hitting him in the chest and propelling him halfway through the open door. The waiting car took off at speed and disappeared into the night but by then, Martin 'House' Malone was dead.

The driver drove at great speed down the roads in a blind panic. What had just happened? One of the men was dead or definitely looked like it, the fleeting moment he saw him. Where was the other one though? He thought he had heard a number of shots about a minute before that last burst so he assumed he was dead too. By the time he reached Crumlin, his stomach was turning at the thought of the inquiry that would certainly be held. He shuddered at the thought of being questioned by the Internal Security unit and even though he was totally innocent of the deaths of his comrades, he had heard horror stories about the 'Nutting Squad" and how they can make you confess to something you didn't even do. As he pulled into the secluded concrete yard by the Camlin River, he literally shook himself as if to be rid of the fears that now seemed irrational and foolish. He quickly set fire to the car and got into another car parked below a row of trees, setting off at speed towards the safe house.

When he arrived, he jumped out of the car and ran inside where he was confronted by Maguire who looked at him expectantly and then over his shoulder in search of McGurran and Malone.

"It all went pear shaped!" the driver gasped. "They were waiting for us! It was a set up! Who knew about this?"

Maguire grabbed the driver and shook him by the arms. "Where are they?" he demanded.

"Dead! Two bursts of gunfire. One of them was blown clean through the open doorway and landed on the door step! I took off out of there as quickly as I could or I would be dead too! You have a tout, mate!"

Maguire stepped back and glared at the driver. He could see the younger man was shaking and obviously in shock. And he could tell that the driver was right in his assertion. There *is* a tout!
Although he was meant to stay in the Crumlin area overnight, Maguire decided, in a rage, to make for Kilrea. On the way there, he was met by RUC land rovers and police cars, lights flashing and sirens wailing like banshees in the night. He guessed that the bridges over the River Bann would be sealed soon so he drove straight to Portglenone at speed to try to cross before the roadblocks were in place. Maguire was sure that if the roadblock was there, they would likely arrest him. He wasn't physically present at the shooting so there would be no witnesses or forensic evidence linking him to it but his past form would be enough for them to arrest him and hold him for a couple of days. That was something Maguire hadn't time for as he had questions to ask and answers to get.

As it happened, he needn't have worried as by the time he reached Portglenone the roadblocks still hadn't been put in place. He drove through the town and then made for Rasharkin where he called at the home of a local Republican sympathiser and demanded the use of her telephone. He then told the woman to ring a number which he dictated, told her who to ask for and the message to give which was:

*"Hugh is here and can't fix the leak. Can you come over straight away as he believes you can help."*

The message concluded with her address and she hung up to make her uninvited guest a cup of tea and some sandwiches. Maguire paced around the living room like a caged animal, trying frantically to make sense of everything that had happened, as he had done since he had left Crumlin an hour ago. He had no appetite for the sandwiches but drank the tea and smoked furiously, flicking the ashes somewhere in the direction of the hearth. Before long, a car stopped momentarily outside the house before taking off again. Within seconds, the back door opened and Jim Bryce entered, nodding briefly to the owner who left the room and went upstairs.

"What has happened, Hugh?" he spluttered. "I have heard something about a shooting and at least two dead!"

"You're asking me what happened!" Maguire bellowed. "The two young boys are dead, that's what happened! The question I have for you is *how* that happened!"

"I took a big risk coming here," Bryce mumbled, looking around the room at nothing in particular. "This will bring a lot of heat so we would need to be very careful for a while."

"Hold on a minute, Bryce!" Maguire stormed. "There are two Republicans lying dead at McCormick's house and you're worrying about 'heat'? I want to know how the Brits knew we were coming for McCormick! He wasn't even there but *someone* was and they took no prisoners. The driver made off from that house like a rocket and, if he has any sense, will never work with us again. What I need to know is how did they know we were hitting McCormick tonight? Who all knew about it and who all did you tell? Belfast will think we are clowns, idiots! Sit down there, Jim, because we have a long night ahead of us."

Bryce sat down heavily trying to make sense of everything. He had spoken to no one about it at all. Not a single person. He was sure McGurran and Malone hadn't spoken out of turn as it would have meant them going to jail or lying dead as they now were. That only left Maguire ….

"I never said a word," he began carefully, knowing the ferocity of Maguire's temper. "The two young boys wouldn't have said anything because they would have been signing their own death warrants. Did *you* maybe mention it, Hugh? Not to the police of course, but maybe to someone in Belfast?"

Maguire glared at Bryce, his eyes starting to bulge with fury. "Are you actually trying to blame me for this? Catch yourself on! I said nothing to no one! I wasn't about to tell Belfast that something *might* be happening in case the whole job was called off. My plan was to go up there today *after* the job was done and tell them then! We need to get to the bottom of this, Jim. We aren't leaving here tonight until we have worked it all out!"

"Well as C/O, and I *am* still in charge here, I am calling off all operations until the leak is plugged" Bryce said thoughtfully. "It's too risky. What am I going to tell the families of them two young chaps? This is a complete and utter disaster! Next time Belfast can clean up their own messes!"

"Don't blame them, Jim!" Maguire snapped back. "We are all in the one thing! I spoke to no one and you say neither did you. The two young fellas were hardly likely to mention it to anyone as it was their necks on the line if it went wrong. Who then? What about that other one? The tea boy?"

"He wasn't even at the meeting when this was arranged," Bryce replied. "In fact he was actually in hospital. He crashed his van and was knocked out so he was kept in overnight. In fact the wife was in the hospital to visit her mother and was going to pop in and see him but the police were there so she never bothered."

"The police?" Maguire asked, suspiciously.

"Aye, well obviously about the accident and all" Bryce came back quickly. "Like, that's not unusual. It was just uniformed ones, not suits."

"Has he been in touch with you since this accident?" Maguire pressed.

"No he didn't get in touch but I called him up this afternoon as he got out this morning. He sounded OK but said he had concussion. He's not an operator, Hugh, but he's all right."

Maguire's eyes narrowed. "You spoke to him and he told you what happened and how he was but 'forgot' to mention his chat with the police?"

"Aw come on, Hugh! He likely never thought anything of it! Sure when we met to chat about the hit he wasn't even there. In fact he was in hospital!"

"No, you're right, he wasn't there but he was there the first time," Maguire said, both to himself and Bryce. "He probably knew we were after McCormick and he could have told the police *that* much. They would then have alerted upstairs and they would have gotten McCormick offside for a while and took over his house in case the hit was imminent. Sorry, Jim, but he's the only one I can think of with enough knowledge and the opportunity to compromise the team. We have to pull him in!"

Bryce sat upright in his chair. "He wasn't even in the meeting, Hugh! He was outside or in the wee kitchen but not in the actual meeting!"

"He has ears, hasn't he?" Maguire snapped back. "He could easily have heard enough and maybe one of them two young lads said something to him that night? Nothing firm but the name of the target. He struck me as weak, that lad. Always moping about with his head down. If the peelers called into the hospital and threatened him with jail over this accident, whom knows what he might have told them to keep himself right? He has to be questioned!"

At length Bryce agreed. He was confident Declan was innocent and it wouldn't be the Nutting Squad asking the questions; it would just be himself and Maguire. They then parted company for the night, Bryce walking down the road to where his lift was waiting and Maguire to Kilrea. Bryce had agreed to pick Declan up and bring him to a house outside Garvagh for questioning.

---

McCormick sat in disbelief as the reports came in from the incident at his home. Smith shared the information he was receiving with his erstwhile colleague and was amused to see the excitement in his eyes and demeanour. McCormick was not known for his emotions so it was refreshing and entertaining to see his mask slip. By dawn, Smith was in possession of most of the facts.

"So what has actually happened?" McCormick demanded to know, as if incapable of believing it all.

"Well, the intelligence was good, Jim, and our friends in the shadows sprung a trap. We haven't got a fix on who they were but I can confirm that a two-man team hit your house and they are both now dead. The driver got away but only to see where he went. He burned the car at a yard not too far from your home and then went to an address in Crumlin. He didn't stay there too long and left alone. Interestingly enough, a short time after he left, one Hugh Maguire also left the house and took off heading north. He definitely went through Portglenone and, as far as I can see, he stopped at a house in Rasharkin."

"He went through Portglenone," McCormick repeated thoughtfully. "Why did they not set up a roadblock on the bridge there?"

"I don't know the answer to that one, Jim, but my guess is that they wanted to see where he went and who he would meet. Also, stop him and do what? He didn't play a central role in the shooting so there would have been no forensics and he would have bluffed off his whereabouts at the time of the shooting had he been stopped. No, I dare say our friends are watching him. Jim, it has been a long night and we need a sleep. I am heading home for a few hours and I need you to give me your word that you will go straight to your hotel and stay there until I contact you."

"I can do better than that, Smithy!" the old McCormick announced. "I will stay right here! Surely you have an empty cell I can lie in for a few hours. No need to lock me in, of course!"

Smith agreed, relieved that McCormick would at least be out of harm's way for a few hours. They parted company after Smith had accompanied McCormick to the cell block. On his way home, Smith wondered what would happen next. Who did Maguire go to in Rasharkin? Were the Special Branch and their help keeping a tight eye on things? Would McCormick survive all of this? When he arrived home and crawled into bed, these questions were still swirling around in his head but the answers continued to be elusive.

About the same time, in his cell bunk, McCormick's paranoid mind tried to find answers to similar questions only he was looking in a very different direction. Why did they let Maguire and the driver run? Were Special Branch really watching them or protecting them? Was the driver – or Maguire – or both of them Agents? If that was the case, would the Branch allow them to take me out eventually? At last he fell asleep but it was a short and fitful one and not one that brought him rest or answers.

-------------------------------------------------------------------

Bryce had decided that he would not fore warn Declan McAleer about the meeting *just in case* there was something the boy was hiding. He remembered McAleer's unease about the shooting of the mechanic and wondered if he *had* been turned at that time. Bryce had heard about cases like that. Something comes along or something happens and Bingo! The conscience can't live with it so you become an informant to wash away guilt and avoid more of the same. He pulled in at the McAleer home and knocked the front door loudly. He was almost surprised when Declan opened it, dressed and all.

"I know you've been through the mill, son, but I need you to come with me and help me with something," Bryce said, sounding apologetic. "It won't take long and there's no danger in it. Come with me now if you can."

Declan had gotten up early to go to the out-patients for a quick check up as instructed the previous day but decided quickly that that could wait. He simply nodded and left the house immediately without even getting a coat. Bryce wondered about this and wondered further if the Branch was somewhere watching them. He knew he was being jumpy and paranoid but after last night, who could blame him? As they drove toward the house near Garvagh, he decided to ask a few questions without Maguire, to see how much Declan knew or was prepared to tell.

"So, no crack then, Declan? Are you feeling all right

after your crash?"

"No crack, Jim," Declan replied quietly. "I am a bit sore and I still have a headache but apart from that, I'm fine."

"How do you think it will go with the police?"

"Oh I will be all right there. It wasn't my fault; the car I swerved to miss was illegally parked."

"Aye I know but you know the police," Bryce continued. "They might try to do you whether it was your fault or not. You know what they're like with folk like us."

"I'll be fine," Declan replied. "No worries there."

Bryce stared at the road ahead and wondered why Declan hadn't told him about the police calling with him and he also wondered at his confidence. *Was he hiding something?* He decided to leave it there and changed tact.

"Have you heard any news today?"

Declan shook his head. "No, why? Have I missed something?"

Bryce didn't reply but pulled into a narrow driveway and indicated that they should leave the car and go inside. Declan wondered why his friend was acting so oddly. It was as if Bryce was trying *not* to say something. As he entered the house, he paused. The living room window was parallel with a window to the back of the house and he saw a car that looked very like Hugh Maguire's. He felt it odd that there would be a meeting with him present but no sign of House or Benny.

"Something wrong?" Bryce asked a little too sharply.

Declan shook his head and followed his mentor indoors. In the living room, Maguire stood alone, looking tired and irritable. The others weren't there. Maguire nodded for them to follow him into a small sitting room at the back of the house. When he stepped into the room, he was shocked and uneasy to find the curtains pulled tight and a small lamp burning in one corner. Bryce walked in past him and Maguire shoved Declan, causing him to stumble.
"So has Jim told you our news, Declan?" Maguire asked immediately. "Sit down there and tell me."

Declan was suddenly terrified. He had no idea what Maguire was talking about but there was no mistaking his hostility and aggressive manner. He looked at Bryce and Bryce looked away.

"No, Jim never told me anything," Declan said, his mouth dry. "He just asked me how I was after the accident."

"Well, let me fill you in! Your two mates, McGurran and Malone are dead! Yep, shot to pieces!"

Declan couldn't believe what he was hearing. It couldn't be true! He sat speechless as Maguire glared at him and Bryce looked inquiringly in his direction. House and Benny dead? How? When? Where? What had happened?

"You look shocked, son!" Maguire said, leaning forward towards him. "Was that not part of the plan, them being killed like dogs? What? Were they just meant to be arrested? And maybe me as well?"

Even though he was still reeling from the news Maguire had given him and even though he was in deep shock, Declan realised what Maguire was implying. He looked at Bryce who stared back passively. They *both* think this was something to do with me!

"Look, I don't know anything at all about this," he said, the panic rising within him. "House and Benny dead? How ..... What happened?"

Maguire then began to tell Declan a sanitised version of what had happened. In fact, he deliberately kept it short to see f Declan might fill in a gap that would prove his guilt. He left out his role and concentrated solely on the account the driver had given. The two men smashed through the door and one was shot dead probably upstairs and the other was blasted clean through the broken door downstairs. Declan listened wide-eyed and in disbelief. This was a horror story! It had to be wrong!

"Not too many people knew the details of this job, Declan," Bryce offered. "We need to know if you overheard anything we spoke about the night you made the tea. Did any of the two chaps tell you what the meeting was about?"

"No" Declan lied. "I heard nothing and no one told me anything. He lied because House had told him the name of the target but such an admission could mean his own death so he decided to deny everything. "Was the hit arranged that night?"

"It doesn't matter!" Maguire yelled. "That's none of your business. If we had been able to trust you then you would have been at the meeting instead of playing housekeeper while the business was being discussed!"

Despite his shock and the physical pain he felt, Declan was stung by the put-down. "It looks to me that it wasn't me who couldn't be trusted! I knew nothing about it and the boys were killed! Why aren't you looking at whoever actually *knew* the details?"

Maguire leapt from his chair and punched Declan on the side of the head and, before Bryce could react, hit him again on the mouth with his other fist. The Commander grabbed Maguire and pulled him back and Declan attempted to stand up but he was too dizzy and his legs buckled below him.

"You were seen talking to the police at the hospital!" Maguire screamed.

Bryce looked at Declan and nodded. "You didn't mention that to me on the phone or on the way over, son."

"There was nothing to mention! They called to see me and asked a few questions about the accident, said the parked car was at fault and then left! They were only there a couple of minutes. If all of this hadn't happened, it wouldn't even have been an issue!"

No one spoke for a time but Maguire's eyes never left Declan. Bryce seemed to be in a world of his own and Declan was still trying to process everything that had been said to him since Bryce had picked him up an hour ago. Finally Bryce spoke.

"Right, we are where we are. The truth is we don't know how this happened. This meeting is over as far as I'm concerned. Declan, I'm taking you home and for the next day or two I want you to stay there. Concentrate on getting better. Hugh, I want you to settle down for the next few days. I have to go and see the two families now and see if they will let the lads have Republican funerals. If they do, I will need you to help me organise them, Hugh. After all that has been taken care of, we will look at this again. One last thing. Until the movement decides otherwise, *I* am the C/O and I expect what I have said to be adhered to, *to the letter.*"

Maguire left first and Bryce helped Declan to the car. On the way back to Swatragh, Bryce spoke.

"You understand why we had to bring you in like that, Declan. When something like this happens, we can't afford to rule anyone out. Me and Maguire had it out last night and I suppose it's only human nature for us to get a bit fraught and uptight. Last night me and him were practically blaming each other so don't take it personal."

"That's all very well but he hates me! And he doesn't trust me at any time, never mind today. And you heard what he said about me being a housekeeper and all."

"Look, Declan, I know you are different from some of the rest of us. You are maybe not as game to be militarily involved as some but you have more brains than most. Maguire has a loud bark and he can bite,too, but he hasn't the brains to take him to the shop for the groceries. In this movement, we need brains as well as brawn. Anyone can pull a trigger but it takes brains to plan a hit or take the movement forward and the Maguires of this world are not capable of either. So what I am saying is that it takes a lot of different folk to make the movement a success. From what I hear, the days of the Maguires are coming to an end. We will be entering a new phase soon and it's folk like you we will need so forget about Maguire."

Declan was pleasantly surprised to hear the Commander saying this; it was a vote of confidence in him, a recognition of the qualities he did possess as opposed to criticisms about his failings. He sat quietly thinking about things. Malone and McGurran were dead; maybe if he had been as fearless as them, he would be lying dead with them or instead of them.

"Thanks, Jim," he said at length. "I believe in the same thing as you and I really do hope the time is coming where I can do something to advance the movement. But I am still worried about Maguire. He's crazy and he has it in for me."

When Bryce had dropped Declan off at home, he paused for a moment to watch him go inside. He drove off and considered things. According to Belfast, there was a very good chance that the entire military campaign was coming to an end. They had been told to ease off their activities and look out men who saw a future in Sinn Fein. McAleer would be ideal, he thought as he drove to the McGurran home. He is clean cut, committed and he has an IRA background so if he joined Sinn Fein, he would keep the 'doves' in their place. And then there was Maguire. For some time Bryce had felt something in his gut every time he met or even thought about him. It was like Maguire always tried *too* hard to prove himself and why? Why not just keep on keeping on without having to come across as a tricolour waver on every occasion? And then there was the question of that young lad who ended up in the River Bann. No one had the opportunity to interrogate him. Maguire had been judge, jury and executioner and the young lad was tossed into the Bann after allegedly confessing to Maguire. But where was the proof? When he had asked that question, the Maguires had accused him of taking the side of an informer so he had backed off. But he had not forgotten…

# Chapter 8

### *Qui Bene?*

Ten hours after Malone and McGurran were shot dead, Sean McDermott was shook awake from a deep sleep. He was initially confused and annoyed at being woke in such a rough fashion. He sat blinking on his bed and tried to work out what was going on. He saw someone whom he vaguely recognised pulling his clothes from a wardrobe and tossing them on to the bed. He only knew the plunderer as Mike.

"You'll have time for some breakfast but then we have to get going," Mike said without offering any explanation for his actions.

"What's all this about?" McDermott demanded, letting his annoyance show.

"While you were counting sheep, two of our lads were shot dead by the Brits," Mike replied shortly. "They were going for the cop who spotted you in Belfast. I don't know much more about it than that but I did know the two young lads who died and they were good ones. Friends of mine, too. The heat is on so I have been told to move you on."

McDermott sensed an unmistakable level of hostility emanating from Mike as he continued to pile articles of his clothing up on the bed. He scrambled out from below the covers and began to dress and, feeling the need to justify himself, decided to clear the air.

"Look, this is the first I've heard any of this. I didn't even know ones from around here were going to be involved in getting McCormick. None of this is my doing though I am genuinely sorry for those young chaps. Were they married?"

Mike shook his head. "Nope! They never lived long enough. Right, after you get a quick wash and breakfast you will be taken through the Sperrins to Strabane. As far as I'm aware, after that you will be moved across the border to Letterkenny until the heat dies down. I don't know a lot about you but you must be something special for two volunteers to lose their lives and all this trouble being taken to keep you safe."

When Mike left the room, McDermott considered his situation. There was no doubting the resentment and anger he had just been subjected to. None of this was his doing yet he felt uncomfortable and guilty. As he got washed, he wished he was back home with nothing to worry about but what clothes to wear. He hoped it wouldn't be Mike taking him to Strabane; that would be a long journey indeed.

After a hasty and less than enjoyable breakfast, McDermott packed his clothes and a few books into two hold-alls and sat in the living room waiting to see what would happen next. Mike had disappeared without explanation and had simply told him to wait in the house until someone called. McDermott hated this house and, as he looked around the sparse room, he felt a sense of relief that he would soon be out of it. He had never been to Letterkenny but he had spoken to volunteers who had stayed in and around Donegal. They told him it was a different world where you could go and do as you please without any fear of being stopped by the police or arrested. He looked forward to such a life and wondered how long he would have to stay in Strabane, hoping it wouldn't be long.

---

As McDermott waited on his lift, McCormick was polishing off an awful breakfast in the police station canteen. Smith hadn't arrived yet and Jim was bored. He wanted to *do something* but what could he do? It was frustrating to think that people were out there actively planning his death and he was acting like an impotent bystander. Checking his watch, he decided to leave the station for a while. He needed a change of clothes but decided not to return to the hotel and chose instead to go into Coleraine town centre and buy some items. His old Polo was parked in the station car park and within minutes he was driving out of the complex on his way to the shops. Why shouldn't I?, he asked himself. It's not like I am under arrest. Anyway he would only be gone for half an hour or so he would likely be back before Smith showed up.

As McCormick left the police station, a car pulled up outside the house where McDermott waited. The driver casually walked up the drive and let himself into the house with his own key. McDermott didn't recognise him at all but that was not unusual as he had never made a habit of running with the Republican crowd. His self defined role within the movement was to apply his talents to the furtherance of the Cause and as such he made himself available to units and areas all over Ulster, preferring to keep company with non-Republicans around home. No one had ever suspected him of being involved although somehow the police had found out something about him and had arrested him once, holding him for three days in Castlereagh Holding Centre. Although he had walked out without any charges being proffered, they had finger-printed him and taken his photograph which he knew they would have retained for future reference.

The driver offered no information about himself and simply told McDermott he was taking him to the car park of a shopping centre on the edge of town where he would be taken further on his journey by someone else. This seemed to be overkill but, McDermott reasoned, these people had just lost two comrades and he knew he was something of a hot potato so he simply nodded his agreement. The driver helped him carry his hold-alls out to the car and they set off in the direction of Limavady to the car park. On the way, McDermott asked if he could stop at a garage and pick up a newspaper and some snacks for the journey. The driver seemed hesitant but McDermott persisted, If the hostility he had experienced from Mike was anything to go by, this was going to be an uncomfortable journey and he intended to avoid conversation with whoever was taking him to Strabane as much as possible.

McCormick tutted with impatience when he noticed that the fuel gage of the Polo was showing he was in urgent need of petrol. It was a strange pet hate of his to fuel his car but the needle was only millimetres from the bottom so, reluctantly, he crossed to the Waterside of Coleraine to get petrol and clock up a few store points for his trouble. Of course the traffic lights were against him and his knuckles turned white with frustration as he desperately wanted to get back to the station before Smith returned. Eventually he was swinging around the roundabout and the petrol station was in sight.

McDermott did not spend long in the garage. He bought some crisps and chocolate and two newspapers. As usual, when you are in a hurry, there is always someone to hold you up and this came in the form of an old woman at the till who seemed at great pains to find her purse in a handbag crammed full of tissues, receipts and other items. Eventually she found it and painstakingly counted out a pile of change to pay her bill. McDermott looked wistfully at an empty till and wondered why no one was at it, keeping the trade flowing. At last he was served and with the very minimum of contact, he left the shop and walked, looking straight ahead, towards the car. He didn't notice the car reversing back towards him to a position by the pumps until the last minute. In shock, he shouted and hit the panel of the Volkswagen Polo and it stopped abruptly. As he walked around the back of the car, he turned to glare at the driver and saw Jim McCormick looking back at him!

McCormick couldn't believe his eyes. McDermott! He jumped out of the car, abandoning it on the forecourt but he was too late. McDermott had jumped in the passengers side of a black Vauxhall Cavalier which took off towards Limavady. Quickly McCormick memorised the number plate: JIW 130. He then ran into the shop and, producing his badge, demanded to use the telephone which the assistant acquiesced to without protest. He immediately dialled the number for Coleraine Police Station and quickly demanded to be put through to Detective Sergeant Martin Smith who answered in seconds.

"Smithy, it's Jim here! Write this down! Black Vauxhall Cavalier, registration number JIW 130."

"Where are you, Jim?" Smith replied evenly. "Not where I left you, that's for sure."

Ignoring his old friend, McCormick continued, "McDermott is in that car, leaving Coleraine and heading in the direction of Limavady! Did you write them details down or will I repeat them?"

Smith started writing immediately, recalling the make, model and registration of the car like the professional he sought to be.

"Yes, yes, I have them. Call me back in three minutes, Jim."

Hanging up the phone he called through to the Divisional Commander and reported the sighting of McDermott, the former assuring him he would take action to apprehend the bomber. He hung up without saying goodbye and seconds later McCormick rang.

"Well, what's happening, Smithy?"

"The Divisional Commander has it in hand, Jim. With SB involvement, we have to go through him as he is liaising with them. Now could you *please* come back here and tell me what has been going on?"

Instead, McCormick decided to tell him right then while on the phone. He suggested that Smith should maybe come and collect him as he could leave the Polo in the forecourt of the garage. They could take a drive by Limavady, maybe he added. Smith didn't argue but instead asked him to come to the police station where they could talk things out. Reluctantly, McCormick agreed and made his way back to the station.

After two or three minutes on the road to Limavady, McDermott blurted out, "That cop back there saw me and I know he recognised me!"

"What cop?" the driver demanded, startled at the revelation. "Where and who?"

"Back there at the garage. It was *him*! It was McCormick! He looked straight at me and I knew looking at him that he recognised me!"

"Is your head right?" the driver shouted angrily. "Why did you not say something sooner? You are becoming a lot more trouble than you're worth!"

They drove on in silence for a mile or so when the driver suddenly swung right into the entrance to a forest.

"Where are we going?" McDermott asked anxiously.

"*I* am going home and you, my friend, are going to wait in here somewhere until I find out what to do next. My orders were to take you to Strabane but that was before we were compromised at the petrol station. I am not taking you another mile in this car. Have you a watch on?"

"Aye, why? You can't just drop me off here! What do you expect me to do?"

"I can indeed just drop you off here, mate!" the driver snapped. "At 7 o'clock this evening, be here at this entrance and someone will come to pick you up. Before you start whining, I know that's hours away but it will take time to get someone to you and we need to give the peelers time to give up chasing you. Make sure and be here at seven."

With that, the driver took off out of the clearance towards the main road on his way back to Coleraine, leaving McDermott standing with his hold-alls and snacks. Less than a mile down the road, the driver saw the roadblock. He had hoped to get back to the town before it had been set up but he was too late. If only that half-wit had spoken up sooner, he thought bitterly. He slowed down knowing it would be futile trying to crash the roadblock. At least if they pull me in, the roads will be clear and that will allow someone the opportunity to collect the man in the forest. He screwed down the car window and in less than two minutes he was out of the car and being handcuffed. As he was shoved into the back of the police car, he realises that he has no way of letting anyone know about the man in the forest. Oh well, he thought, I will have plenty of my own trouble coming so he's on his own.

---

"You have to go back to Belfast," Smith told McCormick after relaying to him that the car he had reported had been stopped and the driver apprehended but McDermott had not been there.

"Are you joking?" McCormick shouted. "All of the

action is here!"

"I think that's the point, Jim. Greer would prefer to have you where he can see you until we find McDermott. Anyway, it looks like he switched cars not long after you saw him so, if it *was* McDermott, he could be on his way back to Belfast for all we know."

"What do you mean 'if it was McDermott'? I would recognise that murdering scumbag anywhere. Anyway he slapped my car when I nearly collided with his so get your white coats out there and dust the car. Boot lid, left hand side. And, while you're at it, you could dust that Cavalier for prints as well. I would bet my life on it that you'll find McDermott's grubby paw prints all over it. You hadn't thought of that! Looks like my place is here, Smithy!"

"The car is being dusted as we speak, Jim, but we will give yours a going over too. Well, I will speak to the Divisional Commander and see if he will intercede with Greer on your behalf. It didn't sound like Greer *wanted* you back, right enough. More like he didn't want you finding McDermott before less volatile officers get to him."

McCormick snorted in disgust. "Greer is a poster boy for Sinn Fein! He works for the politicians, not the Chief Constable. Mind you, having said that, the Chief likely works for them, too. Look, I will get you off the hook and head back up there tomorrow and check in with them. I won't check out of the hotel though, so be prepared to see me again soon."

At McCormick's insistence, Smith pressed for reports on the ongoing interrogation of the suspect, a 24 year-old from Rasharkin. He was proving hard to break and shrugged off questions generally. When told they had a witness that placed McDermott in his car at the garage, he simply replied that he had been heading to a hotel for a bite to eat and picked up a man thumbing a lift who had asked if he could call into the shop at the garage. The driver claimed he had consented to this and then, as he approached the turn off for the hotel, he realised he had forgotten his wallet (the truth being that he kept his money in his pockets and didn't actually own a wallet) so he had apologised to the hitch hiker, let him out of the car and returned to Coleraine where he was stopped at the road block. It was a huge lie and he knew it, the police knew it and both knew each other knew it was a lie; but it couldn't be disproved. That evening Smith was in a position to confirm that there were indeed fingerprints on the side of McCormick's car and also in the Cavalier that matched McDermott's but the driver stuck to his account and, as McCormick packed a few things in preparation for his trip back to Belfast, the Divisional Commander and the local Inspector were conceding that the driver would have to be released the next day without charge.

---

The driver was worried. He had been questioned at

length all of yesterday and he had spent a very restless night in his cell. He guessed it was morning by the sounds he heard; voices shouting, keys jangling and the noises he associated with a changing shift. He felt he had done well to meet each new allegation with an answer but he wasn't sure that he had done enough to win his freedom. The fingerprints were worrying most and he knew his excuse was as thin as paper yet another voice deep in his subconscious told him that although it had been a feeble excuse, they couldn't prove otherwise. His thoughts then turned to the man in the forest. The driver didn't know him at all but the tone adopted by the C/O at his briefing had indicated that he was someone important. He sighed audibly as he thought about the promise he had made to have him collected the previous night. He imagined the man standing in the clearing waiting on the car that never came.

Just then a key was noisily inserted into the lock of his cell door and it swung open, revealing a uniformed officer.

"That's your stay over," the officer said, sounding bored. "Come with me 'til we get you processed and out of here."

The driver nodded and followed the officer, going through the usual formalities that led to his release. He detectives who had questioned him did not appear and the driver left the station wondering if his car had been bugged during the night. He drove into the centre of Coleraine,looking obsessively in the rear view mirror the whole time, checking to see if anyone was following him. Content that he was not being tailed, he pulled into a car park and went to a nearby phone box where he called Mike, asking him to come to a specific cafe in fifteen minutes time. As he waited for Mike to arrive, the driver looked in shop windows giving the impression that he was browsing whereas in reality, he was using the reflection of the glass to ascertain if anyone was watching him. Believing him to be safe, he entered the cafe, positioning himself as a table for two with a clear view of the door. Mile arrived minutes later and the driver ave his account of the previous day.

"You done well," Mike said, patting the driver on the shoulder. "McDermott is more trouble than he's worth! Because of him we can hardly move and there are two dead volunteers! Who benefits from any of this? It would have been better for all of us if he had been caught!"

The driver looked at Mike with obvious surprise. Two dead volunteers? The two young lads shot dead the other day up near Crumlin?

"What will we do about him, though?" he asked at length. "He's up in that forest waiting to be picked up."

Mike nodded,thinking the same thing. At length he said, "You have done your bit. I will get word to our boys in Kilrea and they can get him lifted. He's their problem, not ours. Anyway, after what has happened to you, we will all be under suspicion. OK, you told him he would be lifted at ten last night so,if he has any sense, he will have taken cover when his lift didn't appear and he will likely come to the clearing at ten tonight. His lift will be there and he can get himself away out of our area once and for all. Go home and get a sleep. You done well, mate!"

## Chapter 9

### *The Real Hugh Maguire*

Hugh Maguire sat alone nursing a large glass of whiskey and considered his lot in life. His free hand curled into a fist and his knuckles turned white as he recalled key incidents that had shaped the man he was today. From ever he could remember he had wanted to be a member of the IRA. At primary school, one of his teachers had told them about the Fenians of old and the heroes of the 1916 Rising. These subjects were not part of the curriculum yet they had stayed with Maguire long after geometry and long division had faded from memory. The lessons his teacher had offered back then echoed the stories he had heard from his own father who sang rebel songs every time he's had a few drinks. He would then regale his children with wild tales of mythical Irish heroes and the feats of the Old IRA who had 'driven the Brits out of all but these six miserable counties' and the young Hugh would go to his bed and dream about finishing the work his forefathers had begun.

Throughout his life, Maguire had a quick and violent temper which needed little provocation to manifest itself. Taunts from others at school about his second hand uniform or scuffed shoes were met with rapid punches and vicious kicks. After a few such incidents, his peers learned to leave him alone and most went further by giving him a wide berth altogether. He didn't mind that and felt good about himself, pleased that he could be feared even by older boys. When he left school, Maguire took a job working on a farm near his home. The pay was meagre and the work was hard but as time passed, he developed muscles and fitness which, along with his violent temper, made him a force to be reckoned with. As he toiled on the farm he would day dream about the time when he would strike a blow for Ireland and avenge the Republicans who had given their lives for the old cause of Irish freedom. Totally indoctrinated and fully committed to do whatever it took, he approached an old man, known to have been part of the Old IRA, and asked if he could point him towards someone who would get him into the Provisionals. Of course, no one in his home called them that. The word Provisional was foisted on the section of the IRA that broke away from the movement back in 1970 but it never been their name. Lazy journalism, Maguire had been told; simply a way to describe the 'proper' IRA in order to distinguish it from the 'Stickies' who were, with equal laziness, referred to as the 'Official' IRA.

He recalled with clarity the night he was taken to be sworn into the IRA. It was a ceremony that genuinely moved him but not for the the ceremony itself; but for the fact that he was now part of something that would bring changes his forefathers never managed to secure. Maguire was keen to prove himself to his new comrades so when volunteers were called for, he was first in line. Everyone had been very impressed with his fearlessness and dedication to the cause. He quickly became known as someone you could depend on, someone whose loyalty should never be doubted. Maguire smiled as he recalled the praise and admiration he had received from everyone back then but then grimaced as he remembered when and how it had all gone so wrong.

When the Officer Commanding his local IRA unit was imprisoned, Maguire immediately assumed that he would be granted the position. He could think of no one else as ready and experienced for the role as himself and he let it be known amongst his colleagues that the new Commanding Officer would be him. When the messenger called at his home to given him the time and location of the meeting, he had been ecstatic! Only a week after the arrest of the O/C and they were sending for him to confirm his appointment! As he travelled to the meeting place, he thought about the changes he would make. Changes were needed, he thought as he drove. Bryce will have to go for a start. He was a lazy good-for-nothing and a bluffer with all his big talk and hot air. He was supposed to be the Intelligence Officer for the company but didn't even show any sort of intelligence himself. No, he had to go, Maguire decided. Maybe give him a job selling papers or raising money for prisoners.

When he entered the house he was surprised to see several people there including Bryce. He noticed one man he didn't recognise who seemed to be calling the shots with the others fawning around him. After a few minutes of low conversations and intelligible muttering, the Belfast man called the meeting to order. He introduced himself by offering his first name only and explained that due to certain sensitivities, he had been sent down to confer the position of Commanding Officer. He added that it had not been an easy decision and it had only been made after speaking to the imprisoned former O/C and older Republicans from the area. Maguire had trouble breathing with nervous anticipation, looking from one person to the other as if trying to gauge their reaction to the inevitable announcement.

"So," the Belfast man said, "it's my pleasure to introduce the new O/C; Jim Bryce!"

Maguire felt like he had been punched in the stomach. His legs actually felt weak and he had trouble maintaining his composure. He glared at the Belfast blow-in and then in disbelief at Bryce who was all smiles and red faced. Nice act, Maguire thought bitterly. This had been a set-up! Bryce knew all along he had got the job! Maguire suddenly felt unwell as if his body was incapable of coping with the shock and his insides were struggling to prevent an eruption of fury. Wordlessly he stepped forward and briefly shook Bryce's hand as the latter spoke to the Belfast man and then disappeared outside. As the rain beat down on his face, Maguire still felt like he was boiling with rage. Bryce! A big talking windbag! And that city boy coming down here to lord it over us! Maguire rubbed his face hard, trying to think straight. At length, he pulled himself together enough to pop back inside and nod at the Belfast man before making his excuses to leave.

Maguire shuddered as he thought back on that night. That was the night the Republican movement had let him down and showed itself for the treacherous thing that it had become. For weeks afterwards he had simmered with rage and the resentment within him rose daily. He spent the time trying to work out the reason for Bryce getting the top job and eventually it dawned on him. The militarily inactive Bryce was *exactly* the type of person the leadership wanted to run things at local level. It was no secret that they were nudging towards a ceasefire and the day of the Maguires were coming to an end. The leadership were putting nodding dogs in place all over the country, sheep-like morons who would do the leadership's bidding so that when the ceasefire did come, they would have people in place to ensure the men on the ground were controlled and contained. This was confirmed for Maguire when he heard the new quarter-master was also close to Bryce and the leadership in general. They had played it well, he conceded. They have the men and the weapons neutralised. Still, Maguire was angry and embittered. His anger and resentment festered inside him until he decided to do the unthinkable. It went totally against his nature and belief system but he knew it was the best way to hurt those who had betrayed him and all he believed in; he decided to become an informer.

Taking a swig of his whiskey, Maguire remembered bitterly how it all began. The new quarter-master had moved weapons to a farm building near the village of Upperlands. Maguire knew about the cache because a young volunteer charged with physically moving the weapons had confided in a fellow IRA member who had, in turn, mentioned it to Maguire. Satisfied that enough people knew about it to avoid suspicion landing on him, Maguire went to a phone box in Draperstown and tipped off the police. Within a day, a search of the farm yard and buildings was conducted by the RUC and the weapons were duly found, leading the innocent farmer who genuinely knew nothing about the cache, to be charged with possession of firearms and ammunition. Local people were furious that the farmer had been charged and remanded in custody because of the IRA and the latter were furious because they had lost their weapons and suffered reputational damage from the enraged locals. A witch hunt began to ascertain how the weapons had been and Bryce found himself having to justify his position given that only weeks after his promotion, he had lost half of his arsenal. When asked about the find, Maguire had simply shrugged his shoulders and denied all knowledge of the arms dump, confident that those who had been talking about it would be too afraid to admit speaking out of turn. For some months there was chaos and growing distrust amongst the volunteers as each wondered who the informer had been.

After that, Maguire was hooked. Whatever made Bryce look bad was good for him and he gloated when he saw the O/C shaking his head in despair at meetings, unable to understand how the weapons had been found. It wasn't until a couple of months later that Maguire made contact with the police again. He had been stopped at a checkpoint and became aggressive, threatening the young constable who, with another two colleague, arrested him and took him to Coleraine police station. This time it wasn't Maguire's temper that got him arrested because it had all been an act, an excuse to get inside the police station. From experience, he knew that more often than not, while in custody suspected terrorists would receive a visit from Special Branch officers who would seek to recruit them as informants. Maguire waited in his cell in the hope that this time would be no different and he wasn't to be disappointed. After kicking his heels for a few hours, the cell door opened.

"Well, Maguire!" the Special Branch officer announced. "What are we going to do about this temper of yours? Threatening an officer in the execution of his duties! Hardly the behaviour one would expect from a disciplined Republican like yourself!"

Maguire rolled his eyes as if despairing at the ham fisted attempt by this suited clown to goad him. He knew him quite well having been approached by the oaf on a number of occasions to turn on his comrades. He was a sergeant in Special Branch called McAuley. He then looked the Special Branch man squarely in the eye.

"Listen, let's not go through any stupid charades here. You can charge me with whatever you like but I have a proposition for you." He then took a deep breath. "For my own reasons, which I am not prepared to go into, I am willing to pass you information about Republican activity in the general South Derry area and the Kilrea and Swatragh areas in particular. I won't ever take the stand against anyone in a court case and I don't want any kind of payment. I will work with you and no one else. That's what I'm offering, take it or leave it."

McAuley looked at his old nemesis with a mixture of shock and suspicion. When he had recovered, he pulled the cell door over but not fully closed and sat on the single chair opposite Maguire who remained on the narrow bunk, staring intensely at the cop.

"Am I supposed to be taking you seriously, Maguire?" he asked incredulously. "Is this a trap or some kind of a joke?"

"It's no joke!" Maguire snapped back. "I don't have to prove anything to you but here's something you can check up on. A while ago there a call was made from a phone box in Draperstown tipping you boys off about an arms dump outside Upperlands. You boys followed up on it and found weapons and ammunition. The farmer who owned the property was charged with possession and remanded in custody though I heard he got bail. That farmer knew nothing about them guns. I know because I made the call. Go ahead and check it out."

McAuley paused a few moments and then exhaled loudly. He knew about this incident and, at the time, he was furious because he had wanted to bug the weapons and catch the IRA team red-handed on an operation but he had been over ruled. It seemed to McAuley that the 'war' against Republicans had been wound down and now, rather than take them out, the security forces were content just to hamper them. He looked at Maguire unblinkingly.

"You're serious!" he spluttered. "I am not sure if we can do it your way, though. This is the RUC, after all, so there has to be some kind of paperwork."

"No chance," Maguire replied firmly. "It's my way or no way and if you knock me back, we never had this conversation and we never will again."

McAuley made an excuse to leave the cell for a few minutes and used the time to look at his options. This, he decided, was like manna from Heaven. Maguire was a born killer and here he was, for whatever reason, offering to cripple the IRA in South Londonderry! The decision was easy and McAuley returned to the cell telling Maguire he had a deal. Before he left, he gave Maguire a number to contact him on and offered to get the charge of threatening an officer dropped. Maguire refused the offer, asking only if it could be reduced to Disorderly Behaviour which, as a minor offence, would merit only a fine or a conditional discharge. McAuley agreed and within the hour Maguire was released from custody having been charged with Disorderly Behaviour.

With Bryce at the helm, Maguire knew there wouldn't be much information to pass on to McAuley yet the weekly gatherings continued with Bryce holding court and trying to sell the volunteers the latest notions coming from Sinn Fein in Belfast. Although he said little, Maguire despised these meetings and the clear pro-peace message being conveyed by the O/C. Whilst paying lip service to all of this, Maguire had made his own contacts in Belfast through his brother, Joey, and these weren't Sinn Fein apologists but were *real* Republicans who wanted to keep the war going. He decided not to let the locals know of his growing number of contacts in Belfast in case it would give rise to jealousy or ferment fears from the notoriously insular Republicans of South Londonderry. So, when Bryce summoned hi to meetings, he went along and passed the time with apparent interest but, in reality, seeking how he could hurt those with him.

As he poured another whiskey, Maguire recalled with horrific clarity the one event in his life that he would never come to terms with. It had been discussed at a special meeting called by Bryce. A part-time UDR man living near Maghera had come to the attention of the IRA. He was a member of the Orange Order and had been openly hostile to Republicans when stopped at roadblocks so the decision had been taken to shoot him dead. Maguire made no offer to be part of the unit selected for the operation, scheduled to take place the following Saturday evening, so a three man team was chosen from amongst those present. Maguire knew all three of them and listened quietly as Bryce gave them instructions. A 'friend of the movement' was employed in a hotel in Ballymena and had taken a booking for a birthday party for the UDR man's wife. The target had made the call and the date had been set for the Saturday evening. The woman had recognised the name of the caller who supplied his address and phone number and she had passed these details on to a friend who passed them to Bryce. Maguire chuckled to himself when he heard this; typical of Bryce not to have known about the UDR man until this piece of information had come his way. He likely added that bit about him being aggressive at roadblocks to somehow justify the hit instead of just ordering it because the man was a member of the security forces!

Two days before the planned hit, Maguire placed a call to McAuley and gave him what information he had, including where and when the shooting would take place (the car park of the hotel as soon as the UDR man arrived) and who would be carrying out the hit (two young men from Kilrea and a driver from

Bellaghy). Maguire sought assurances that the police would only arrest the three and that there would be no casualties to which McAuley replied indignantly that they were guardians of the law, not assassins like the IRA. When he replaced the receiver, Maguire was surprised to find that he felt no guilt whatsoever. He had become consumed with contempt for Bryce and the IRA in general as they seemed more and more reluctant to plan operations against the British, preferring instead to advocate the genius of Sinn Fein and the wisdom of engaging in politics to achieve their aims.

On the Saturday evening, Maguire felt a strange thrill of nervous excitement as he waited to hear the news from Ballymena. He checked his watch and noted that in an hour's time, it would all be over. The three young men would be in cells somewhere and Bryce would surely be finished. Unable to settle, he decided to visit his brother, Joey, a committed Republican who would later vouch for the shock and horror felt by both of them when the news eventually reached them. He pulled up at Joey's house about half an hour before the planned hit and was surprised to find his brother was not at home.

"I'm sorry, Hugh, but Joey isn't here," Justine Maguire told her brother-in-law. "He hadn't planned to go out the night but a young chap called for him about an hour and a half ago and he went away somewhere with him. I don't know where he went but he's maybe away to see Jim Bryce."

"Bryce?" Maguire asked startled. "Why do you think he's away to see him?"

"Well, he phoned about fifteen minutes before that young chap called and asked Joey if he was free for a couple of hours."

Maguire felt the bile rise in his stomach and quickly made his excuses and left. Please, he thought, don't let this be what I think it is! Don't tell me our Joey has been brought in on this job! He jumped in his car and sped towards Bryce's house, trying to work out what to say on the way as he couldn't afford to look suspicious in the aftermath of it all. As he raced along the narrow roads, it dawned on him that he would be drawing unnecessary attention to himself if he went to Bryce's home so he pulled his car over to the side of the road and waited, a thousand thoughts crashing around inside his head.

The next morning Justine called him in great distress to tell him that Joey and two others had been arrested the previous night as they entered a car park in Ballymena. Within a few days, Maguire had been able to piece together enough of that night's activities to make sense of what had happened. The designated driver claimed to have taken ill and wasn't able to perform his necessary task in pursuit of the UDR man. Joey Maguire had been chosen to replace the driver on the operation and had left that evening to take the gunmen on their journey to and from the hotel. When they entered the car park in a stolen car, the whole place was suddenly illuminated by glaring floodlights and their only exit was blocked by an unmarked police car. Before the IRA unit knew what was happening, armed policemen appeared from nowhere, their guns trained on them. Knowing there was no way out, the IRA unit surrendered their weapons and were duly arrested, handcuffed and taken away to Castlereagh Holding Centre in Belfast. Maguire was in absolute turmoil as he considered his role in the arrest and subsequent imprisonment of his brother but his instinct for survival took over and he arrived at Bryce's home claiming there was an informer at work and demanding a swift investigation. The hapless Bryce had no choice but to agree and asked Maguire to take the lead in establishing the identity of the informer.

Maguire knew he had to move quickly, both to shift the blame onto someone else but also to ease the pain of his own guilt. He called regularly with Justine, giving her money and groceries, each time swearing that he wouldn't rest until the informer responsible for her husband's imprisonment had been found and punished. Maguire had never liked Brendan Flynn. He was a brash, cocky loudmouth who talked a good fight but had done little to justify the belief he had in himself. He had been at the meeting when the plans had been made to shoot the UDR man but he hadn't volunteered. In fact, Maguire had noticed that when Bryce had asked for volunteers, Flynn had kept his eyes firmly on the ground, careful *not* to draw attention to himself. So, Flynn would be no loss to the Republican movement and few would doubt that he had been the informer. Maguire had heard others disparage the young man and the general feeling was that he wanted to wear the badge without doing the job of sheriff.

For the next few weeks, Maguire directed a whispering campaign against Brendan Flynn. He visited Joey in prison and convinced him that Flynn had known the details of the hit so it might well be him. He also pointed out that the volunteer who had created the arms dump at the farm in Upperlands was a close friend of Flynn's. What if the young fellow had told Flynn about the arms dump? Was it not suspicious that Flynn had managed to avoid doing much? What about his swaggering manner that he used to convince others that he was something he was not? The force of Maguire's argument convinced Joey who was looking for someone to blame anyway. Having established the 'guilt' of Flynn with his brother, Maguire moved on to other IRA members in the South Londonderry area and found fertile ground for his seeds of doubt. Soon he had convinced almost everyone that Brendan Flynn was an informer. He didn't, however, run it past Bryce because he wanted others to do that because, down the line, Bryce wouldn't be able to pin the blame on Maguire, should Flynn somehow be exonerated posthumously.

Maguire knew he couldn't risk Flynn being brought in

for questioning wither by locals or the Internal Security unit. There was a chance they would find him not guilty and then they would go looking for the *actual* informer. So, he convinced his family and Joey in particular that it was pointless going to the IRA for justice as they had allowed Flynn to inform on his colleagues for ages without working out he was doing it. So, Hugh Maguire took it upon himself to deal with the problem and he did so with the cunning for which he was notorious.

Rather than use a telephone, Maguire drove to near the Flynn home and waited for Brendan to leave the house to go to work. Within minutes, he spotted the young man leaving the yard and walking along the road for his lift. Maguire drove up alongside him and told him he was needed for a meeting that evening at 6pm and that Bryce had ordered the meeting to discuss the way forward. Flynn readily agreed to be present and Maguire added that, due to security issues following the arrests in Ballymena, the location of the meeting would not be revealed until shortly before it. He instructed Flynn to take his own car to the Agivey bridge near Aghadowey and park it in the small car park beside it where he would be collected. Flynn nodded and Maguire told him to be there at 5.30pm but to tell no one as only a select few had been asked to attend. Maguire knew this would appeal to Flynn's vanity thus guaranteeing his silence.

That evening, Flynn was already in the car park

when Maguire arrived, the latter gesturing the younger man to join him in his car. They drove towards Garvagh, turning left in the direction of Kilrea. Flynn remained quiet for the duration of the journey until they reached a small wooded area on the banks of the Bann just outside Kilrea. Maguire pulled in and said the meeting was being held in the actual wooded area as a security precaution and they both left the car and began walking along a narrow path alongside the fast moving river with Flynn to the fore. Maguire then reached inside his jacket and removed a claw hammer and, as Flynn asked how much further they had to go, Maguire swung the hammer hard, smashing it into the side of Flynn's head. The younger man staggered for a moment and Maguire struck him a second time, rendering his victim unconscious. Setting the hammer down, Maguire then rolled the limp body into the river and watched as it disappeared in the fast current. He then wiped his fingerprints off the hammer with a cotton handkerchief and threw it with all of his strength into the river on his way back to the car.

Early next morning, Maguire was awakened out of his sleep by Bryce pounding on the back door. The Commander was visibly shaken as he revealed that a body had been retrieved from the River Bann an hour before and that it was Brendan Flynn. He went on that Flynn's family had contacted him late the previous night wondering if had seen him. Flynn's father had then called him again about twenty minutes ago to tell him his son had been found in the Bann near the Castleroe.

"I have been told by a number of folk that you were fingering him for the tout who put Joey and the boys in jail," Bryce stated accusingly.

"Aye, that's right!" Maguire snapped. "Think about it, Jim! He never volunteered for anything yet always wanted to know everything! He knew all the details of the job Joey and the boys were on and he was close to the young fellow who hid the arms on the farm at Upperlands. And, as well as all that, he was always giving it Jack-the-Lad as if he was something. It all adds up to him being a tout, Jim! But, if it makes you breathe any easier, I know nothing about his death. I was here all evening watching TV but my guess is that he heard the chat and knew his number was up so, to avoid meeting up with Internal Security, he jumped into the Bann. The noose was tightening around his touting neck so he took the only option open to him."

They spoke for a few minutes more and then Bryce left to go and offer some comfort to the Flynns. As he drove along the road, there were two things he knew for sure; Maguire had murdered young Flynn and no one would ever get Maguire to admit it. Later that day, when they found Flynn's car parked at the Agivey bridge, Flynn had reached two conclusions; the young man had parked his car by the Bann and jumped in or Maguire had planned this very carefully and would never stand before a court to answer for it.

But that was all a long time ago, Maguire thought as he swallowed the last of his second glass of whiskey. Since then he had been exceptionally careful in his dealings with McAuley. He had passed him mainly low grade information about things that couldn't be traced back to him. Tonight he had to go and rescue that McDermott from the forest up off the Limavady Road. The movement was in trouble, he thought bitterly. They can't even get one on-the-run volunteer out of the way! Pulling on his coat, he left the house, slamming the door angrily behind him.

# Chapter 10

### *Joining The Dots*

McCrum was pleasantly surprised to get the call from Joe McNamee and, taking the usual precautions, met him at the ASDA car park as agreed.

"To what do I owe the pleasure, Joe?" McCrum asked as the Republican settled in the passenger seat of the car.

"Hot goss," McNamee replied in his normal deadpan manner. "Things are changing with us big time. I'm sure you have noticed there has been a lot less action of late and some of our men have been given other jobs to do. Anyhow, I got a promotion of sorts and they are using me as a driver these days. Now, I drive several ones around but there's one in particular who might interest you. Josey McCloy."

McCrum recognised the name straight away and couldn't help but look surprised at the revelation. McCloy was a big name in Republican circles, regarded as a hawk with a strong affinity with the hard line elements.

"Of course you're wondering how I got a job like this. Well the truth is I don't drink, I have a licence and I have been questioned by your colleagues and never had a conviction. They see me as useful and trustworthy. So, even though I drive others now and again, it's mainly McCloy. You would be surprised at how loose with the tongue he can be. I don't think it's because he's got a big mouth, though; I think it's because I ask no questions, never interrupt and do exactly what I'm told. He is relaxed with me driving and feels he can talk freely."

McCrum nodded, seeing the wisdom of this and waited expectantly for McNamee to finish his story.

"Well, it would seem that McCormick's friend McDermott is causing headaches. McCloy speaks to others in the car about these things and never me but I have ears and I can hear what's being said. Anyway, McCloy was in a real bad temper yesterday, ranting about McDermott. He said he went to a meeting arranged by some boy Maguire up in South Derry somewhere to arrange for McCormick to be taken out to protect McDermott but they had made a real cock-up of it and two young fellows had been shot dead. Now it seems they have McDermott somewhere but they don't know what to do with him and the police are crawling all over South Derry looking for him and there's a very real risk that they will find arms and so on."

"Who was he telling this to and where is McDermott at?" McCrum asked, the excitement building inside him.

"Just some old fellow Jim from up the country

somewhere," McNamee replied. "He never called him by his surname so I don't know it. As for McDermott, I couldn't tell you because this Jim didn't know either."

"This is very valuable information, Joe!" McCrum exclaimed, already planning how he would use it.

"Oh that's not the end of the matter," Joe replied ominously. "According to Jim, the Maguire Josey mentioned at the start might be working for you boys! Aye, I think that's how it went. Jim said he was worried about this Maguire because stuff had gone missing over the last few years and Maguire's brother got caught going on a job and jailed. According to this Jim, Maguire went on a rampage, really over- the-top and found a young lad he believed to be the tout and killed him without it being sanctioned. Jim said he couldn't do much about it as this Maguire denied it all and there was no proof but he's convinced he did it. Now McDermott is up there somewhere and folk are being arrested wholesale. That's it. That's everything I know."

"Can you say it all into a tape?" McCrum asked, producing a small recorder.

McNamee shook his head. "No chance, mate! You aren't getting my voice on anything that can come back to haunt me. *You* say what I just told you into your tape recorder and I will listen. If you make a mistake, I'll put up my hand, you stop the tape and I will tell you the right way of it and you can start again."

McCrum agreed and, after only one interruption, they concluded the conversation and parted company, McCrum giving his informant an envelope containing money which surprised McNamee who was more used to McCormick's meanness. McCrum was delighted with the information he had been given and determined to see McCormick that night even if it meant driving to Coleraine. However, as he pulled up at his home to get changed, he saw the Volkswagen Polo in his drive and knew that he wouldn't have to find McCormick as he had found him.

"What brings you back to the Big Smoke?" McCrum asked the grinning McCormick who was enjoying a cup of coffee with Alison.

"Orders, mate!" McCormick said breezily. "Greer and Bryson realised they can't live without me and ordered me back to say hello. Anyway, I arrived back this afternoon and met Greer who warned me that my life is in danger and told me to let my colleagues do their job without hindrance or any interference from me. Of course I agreed which was easy as I am not one for hindering or interfering with investigations."

McCrum raised his eyebrows to denote his disbelief at this claim and took a seat as Alison left to fetch him a coffee. Having drained his cup, McCrum became agitated by his wife's continued presence.

He was desperate to share the information he had gleaned with his colleague but felt uneasy about discussing anything in front of Alison. Eventually he rose quickly from his chair and motioned for McCormick to follow him to a little den to the back of the house. Once settled, McCrum recounted his conversation with McNamee as McCormick sat transfixed, drinking in every single word.

"Play the tape, John!" he snapped, his excitement rising.

McCrum pushed the play button and listened to his own voice coming back to him. He had to play the tape four times before McCormick was satisfied, falling back into his seat as if overwhelmed by it all.

"Do you know any of these people, Jim?" McCrum asked, hoping he did.

"Oh aye, I know them all right! McCloy, as you likely know, is a hard hitter from up here. I had no idea he was involved in all of this! Maguire is a bit of a legend up there where legends are few. He's a killer and of that I am certain but *an informer*? I find that hard to swallow. The 'Jim' might well be Jim Bryce who was definitely in the IRA when I was based in Coleraine but he wasn't much of a mover and shaker so it might not be him McCloy spoke with. I can't remember anyone being killed up that way for being an informer but I will check all these things out. Can you make me a copy of that tape to take with me?"
"Certainly," McCrum replied happily. "I will do it right

now. Take where, if you don't mind me asking?"

"Up to Coleraine! I will be in Smithy's living room before you have your electric blanket switched on!"

Slightly over an hour later, true to his word, McCormick was sipping a mug of hot coffee ad Smith listened to the tape, making notes on a pad in his own efficient way. When he had listened to the tape twice, he turned to McCormick smiling.

"I think I can make sense of all of this and of most things that have happened since you saw McDermott in the street that day in Belfast. McDermott is a valuable asset of the IRA and they need his expertise. When it was clear that you had recognised him that day, he must have appealed to the Belfast boys to take you out or perhaps he simply mentioned that he had met you and they decided to take you out to protect their prized resource. Either way, they must have contacted the IRA in South Londonderry which makes sense as McDermott lives in this general area. The main man in organising the hit is this man McCloy whom you say is a main mover and shaker up there in Belfast. The main contact *here* is Maguire who I believe is Hugh Maguire, a psychotic Republican from Kilrea. The 'Jim' is undoubtedly Jim Bryce who we believe is the commanding officer of the area covering Kilrea and Swatragh. Now, judging by this conversation, Jim Bryce suspects Maguire of being an informer and I for one agree. He seems to be a law onto himself and he does seem to have some kind of immunity from imprisonment. We have suspected for some time that he is working for Special Branch and that would tie in with what Bryce said here. Now, there aren't too many murders in this part of the world but there was one which I believe is the one referred to in the tape. A young fellow, Brendan Flynn, was fished out of the River Bann some time ago. He was a Republican and was accorded a paramilitary funeral. His family claimed he had fallen into the river as they couldn't accept any other explanation and we suspected suicide but when the post mortem was carried out, they detected a serious brain injury like he had been assaulted with a heavy blunt instrument. Also, there was water in his lungs so he did die from drowning. Our theory? Flynn was knocked unconscious and then thrown into the river to drown. This is undoubtedly the person Bryce was referring to in the tape. Now it looks like Maguire was the killer and we never thought of that. Very interesting indeed."

They discussed the events that had unfolded since the murder of John Hargy and the contents of the tape for over an hour and it became clear that the intrigue and cycle of violence that had been unleashed could only by ended by one of two things; the apprehension of McDermott or the elimination of Jim McCormick.

"Oh, I forgot to tell you!" Smith exclaimed, unusually excited. "We had a visitor at the station today and he was asking to speak to you. Your old mate from back in the day; Harry Bradshaw!"

McCormick stared back at his colleague in confusion. Harry Bradshaw? What on earth did that washed up old goat want? McCormick reflected on his last meeting with Bradshaw and recalled the level of hostility the old man had directed at him. And now he was looking a chat ……..

"OK, lets go!" McCormick said, louder than he had intended to.

"Go where? Jim, it's almost midnight!"

"We are going to see what my old mate wants, Smithy! A friend in need and all that! Grab your coat mate; we don't want to keep old Harry waiting!"

Twenty minutes later McCormick and Smith were at Harry Bradshaw's front door, McCormick pounding it loudly with his fist.

"Harry always did love 'the peelers knock'. This will get him out of bed in a flash! Wait to you see the face on him, Smithy!"

Sure enough the hall light blinked on and moments later the door opened. Harry Bradshaw stood looking dishevelled before them in a dressing gown loosely tied, his bony legs appearing unsteadily beneath it.

"I hear you were looking a catch-up, Harry!"

McCormick bellowed, pushing past the old man and letting himself into the small kitchen. "Well, I know how impatient you are so I came as soon as I heard. So, what can you do for me?"

Bradshaw glared at McCormick and then eyed Smith with contempt. "Don't think you're bringing him along to reel me back in when you go back to Belfast. I am done with the lot of you and I told you that, McCormick!"

"Smithy just gave me a lift here, Harry. I am happy for you to enjoy your retirement! Anyhow, I heard it was you who was looking for me so I am just hear responding to your request for an audience."

Bradshaw scowled back and sat down on a convenient stool. "This might be nothing but I have been watching the news and I know you boys are looking for a Republican who's on the run or something." He paused and McCormick looked enquiringly at Smith who nodded, confirming that the press office had indeed issued a statement naming McDermott and asking people to be vigilant as he was believed to be in the North Coast and may be armed and dangerous. Just to see if we could flush him out, Smith added almost apologetically.

"Anyway!" Bradshaw snapped irritably. "I was up in the forest yesterday evening walking the dog, one of the few pleasures left to me. Well, I was walking along one of them wee paths,go in the Limavady Road entrance and take the first path to the left, and

I saw someone among the trees. He was a thin faced man and had either hold-alls or two wee suitcases. When he saw me, he grabbed the luggage and went on into the trees. On the way back, I had a wee nosey and seen the remains of a wee fire. It looked to me that it had been lit to keep someone warm and the grass around it was all flattened like someone had been lying there. It might be nothing but I thought I would let you know."

Immediately McCormick sprang forward and, completely ignoring Bradshaw, shouted at Smith in small, excited sentences.

"That day I saw him! That day I saw him at the garage! He got into that car and it took off for Limavady! And you set up roadblocks, remember? The car was stopped no time later heading back *in* to Coleraine! The driver dropped him off *in the forest! That's why he disappeared off the radar!* We were looking for him on the *roads* and he was actually in the forest! When was that? Two days ago and he was still there yesterday evening! We need to get a team into that forest Smithy!"

Smith nodded suggesting that they should go there immediately and he would call in support from his car radio. McCormick began to head for the door and then paused.

"Why are you helping me, Harry?"

Bradshaw laughed bitterly. "Simple, McCormick,

because as much as I hate the sight of you, I hate Republicans more. Now go and get him, if it *is* him and remember; take no prisoners!"

McCormick smiled broadly and waved as he left, following Smith to the car. Within minutes, they were on their way to the forest, Smith having radioed in for additional support and roadblocks on all roads leading to and from the entrance.

---

Just as McCormick arrived at Smith's home to play him the tape, Hugh Maguire arrived at the entrance to the forest on the Limavady Road. The few whiskeys he had before he left the house had neither calmed him nor curbed his temper. He shouldn't be doing this, he concluded, and he was bitter about being relegated to the role of chauffeur for some big shot the city boys couldn't do without. He checked his watch and it blinked the numbers 21.55. Again Maguire tormented himself by reflecting on how pointless this was. He didn't even know if this McDermott would even show up because he was to be collected the previous night! Maguire didn't believe in luck; he believed in careful planning and nothing about this was planned. It was all reactionary and that carried with it an element of risk. He knew he had protection from Special Branch but that wouldn't help him if he was stopped at a roadblock without blowing his cover. He turned off the ignition and waited in the dark, hoping it wouldn't be long until McDermott appeared. Either way, he would wait until quarter past ten and then he was out of here. McDermott would be on his own.

The opening of the passenger door nearly gave Maguire a heart attack. He had been so consumed with his own thoughts that he hadn't noticed the man approach his car from behind. He recovered visibly yet his heart was still pounding as McDermott threw his luggage into the back of the car.

"You took your time!" McDermott snapped. "I have been waiting here in this jungle for nearly two days!"

"You're lucky I came at all!" Maguire replied angrily. "I am taking you to a safe house for the night until we can work out what to do with you. Now sit back and shut up and give me peace to think!"

Maguire's aggression was enough to guarantee McDermott's silence. Maguire had already decided to take his passenger to that wee house young McAleer had found, ironically the same place where they had first planned the shooting of the cop, McCormick, in a bid to save this idiot's life. On his way to the forest, he had thought about arranging for McDermott to be arrested by way of a tip-off to McAuley. But it couldn't be tonight, not when he was the driver nor could it be at the safe house as he was the only one who knew that that's where he was taking McDermott. No, in the morning he would go and tell Bryce where McDermott had been secreted and then he would pick his moment. It was imperative that Bryce would be implicated and regarded as a suspect when McDermott was found. That would see the end of him and naturally Maguire would be the natural successor. He would turn South Derry upside down and show the whole country what war was like! Aye, he concurred with himself, McDermott was his ticket to the big time!

The cottage was dark and cold but Maguire showed some degree of hospitality by helping to prepare a fire. When it was lit, he sat down and lit a cigarette, looking at McDermott through the drifts of smoke.

"Not exactly the Ritz but it beats sleeping below a tree," he muttered.

"Only just," replied McDermott. "Hey, I think I know you! You're a Maguire from Kilrea, aren't you? I remember meeting you before. We were never introduced but you were at things I was also at and I asked who you were. Joey Maguire?"

"No, Joey's my brother, down in Long Kesh doing time because of a tout called Flynn," Maguire said convincingly. "I am Hugh and it's not normally my job to ferry people about so count yourself privileged. So tell me, McDermott, why is the world and his dog really after you?"

"Call me Sean. Look, I never wanted all this attention or to cause everyone all this hassle. When I was in Coleraine, the ones there treated me like a leper and you're attitude hasn't been too comforting. My only 'crime' was to be seen by that cop McCormick on a street in Belfast. He recognised me and stopped me. I gave a false name but he obviously worked out who I was and that set off a chain of events I had no control over. I am not that important, Hugh, but I never asked for all this carnage to follow me. It eats at the insides of me when I think of them two young chaps who were shot dead at McCormick's house. The whole thing is a disaster! I saw him, too. He's up in this area. That's how I ended up in the forest. He's like a dog with a bone and he will never give up until either me or him are dead."

"I knew the two young fellows," Maguire replied quietly. "I took them up to that job and waited for them in a safe house. I honestly don't know how that happened and that's why only you and me and the C/O will know where you are. It will either be me or him who takes you on the rest of your journey because there's a tout up here and until we find out who it is, everything will be kept strictly on a need-to-know basis."

Maguire then left McDermott and on his way home, he chuckled at his own genius. When the police put him away, he will know that it had to have been me or Bryce who tipped them off and I risked everything going to collect him so that will rule me out. It will look like Bryce spoke out of turn to someone and got them both caught! Now to call with big bad Bryce to let him know everything and get him to arrange for someone to collect McDermott in the morning.

Smith and McCormick did not stay long at the forest. Within minutes of their arrival, the reinforcements came and they quickly established that a set of fresh tyre marks in the muddy clearance indicated that a vehicle had been there a short time ago. The forensics team then arrived and began erecting huge spotlights whilst other officers bearing torches began scouring the paths leading into the forest. Smith checked his watch and then motioned to McCormick to follow him to the car which McCormick did under protest.

"We have a call to make, Jim, and I don't want any arguments. It's now 11.25pm and those boys know their job so I think it best to leave them to it while we go see the boss."

"Boss? What boss?"

"The Divisional Commander, Jim. We have joined many of the dots but there are still some things that don't add up. We need to brief him and have him on our side plus it will do no harm to keep him appraised even if it's just to cover our own backs."

"Maybe I will just wait in the car, Smithy." McCormick replied chuckling. "He never liked me when I was stationed up here so I doubt if he'll want to see me at this hour of the night, never mind with all of this going on! Do you know where he lives?"

"Yes I do, Jim. We play a lot of golf together and we have had dinner in each others homes."

McCormick laughed incredulously. "Well! I am sure he was glad to see you replacing me! Golf, eh? Still an Englishman after all these years!"
In no time, they were parked on the roadside in front of a spacious two story house and, closing the car doors quietly, they walked up the drive and Smith rang the doorbell.

"Why did you insist on us closing the car doors so quietly if we are going to wake him up anyway?" McCormick asked, goading his colleague.

"Just let me do all of the talking, Jim," Smith replied, ignoring the question. "Don't speak unless you are asked a question and even then, let your answer be short and delivered politely. This man is my friend as well as my superior and I would like us to remain friends after you have returned to Belfast."

Before McCormick could think of a response, the hall lit up and the Divisional Commander opened the door with a flourish.

"What on earth? Why are you here at this time of night, Martin? And what is *he* doing here?"

"Perhaps we could speak inside, DC," Smith replied apologetically.

Begrudgingly the Divisional Commander bade them

enter his home and showed them into a spacious and comfortable living room.

"His bath robe cost a lot more than Bradshaw's," McCormick hissed. Smith frowned back and put his finger to his lips and McCormick sighed audibly in exasperation.

As quickly as possible, Smith recounted everything to his superior who listened intently. Smith then played McCrum's tape and the Divisional Commander frowned as he took in every word spoken. It took a good 20 minutes to appraise the boss and, in fairness to McCormick, he managed to sit quietly as if to prove that he could follow orders if he felt he had to.

"I must say, this is great police work!" the Divisional Commander said as Smith clicked the stop button on the tape player. "It would seem that your enthusiasm hasn't waned since last we met, McCormick but I am not sure if any of this will stand up in court. The officer who speaks on the tape will obviously not want his source exposed and I doubt very much if our friend McDermott is still at large in the forest. Now, in light of the information you have given me, I regret allowing Special Branch to take the lead role in all of this. They obviously 'run' Maguire and he is now under suspicion from his own kind. I think it's high time we introduced proper policing, the emphasis on *proper*, Mr McCormick. Now, let me think about this and see where we go."

Before the Divisional Commander had a chance to think or do anything, his telephone shrilled loudly behind him. He sighed as if wondering what else this night would bring. McCormick and Smith pretended not to listen as the chief spoke rapidly down the receiver, pausing only to listen to the caller on the other end. He was just out of earshot but both his guests heard him concluding the call with the words, "I will be in directly. Give me 20 minutes to change into my clothes."

"Well, men!" he exclaimed. "It looks like it's all happening now. McDermott is in the abandoned cottage where they hatched the plot to have you murdered, McCormick. As you know, Special Branch took control of the operation there and they had very effective bugs installed. The deal was that they could do that but all and any information gleaned must be shared with us. It seems that our Mr Maguire arrived at the cottage a little while ago and we have a recording of his conversation with Sean McDermott. The caller there just told me that Maguire has left McDermott there for the night and has gone home. Although this is highly irregular, you may join us at the station McCormick. If nothing else at least we will know where you are. Martin, can you take us all there in your car. I will be down in a few minutes." Without waiting for an answer the Divisional Commander disappeared upstairs and McCormick and Smith looked at each other wide-eyed. Whatever next indeed!

# Chapter 11

## *Closing the net*

When the three of them arrived at the police station, it was a hive of activity with uniformed officers, plain clothes officers and civilian workers going from place to place along the maze of corridors. The Divisional Commander had arranged for a meeting of all relevant officers in his huge office upstairs.

"McCormick, although you have no jurisdiction here, because of your inadvertent involvement in all of this you may attend the meeting but only as an observer. Again, as an *observer*. You may be asked to speak should it be deemed that your intricate knowledge of the case would be helpful but otherwise, your absolute silence would be appreciated."

McCormick nodded, agreeable only because he was keen to hear what the plan would be to bring the whole saga to an end. As they ran up the stairs, the larger-than-life McAuley stood, beetroot faced at the top, obviously exhausted. He looked down on the officers ascending the stairs and his visage changed completely.

"McCormick!" he shouted between gasps. "What is *he* doing here? I hope he's not going to the meeting as that would be a massive conflict of interest!"

McCormick beamed at him. "Massive. An interesting word coming from you, Jim. I see you're still wearing the same suit as you were wearing eight years ago. You must have paid good money for it."

McAuley's face turned a strange shade of purple and he glared at the Divisional Commander who moved quickly to diffuse the situation.

"McCormick will be present as an observer and will only speak if and when called upon to do so. Come on, let's go! We don't have time to waste."

The meeting began soon afterwards and although the Divisional Commander was open and forthright in his reporting of recent events, McAuley seemed reluctant to confirm or deny anything unless pressed upon to do so. McCormick deliberately smirked at him every time their eyes met which left McAuley flustered and agitated. It was agreed that they would keep the cottage under close observation for the rest of the night and that when someone came to collect McDermott in the morning, they would swoop.

"Whatever happens, if the driver turns out to be Hugh Maguire, he is not to be touched!" McAuley blurted out. "We have a special interest in him."

The Divisional Commander looked sternly at the Special Branch man. "Is that a request? If so you may wish to rephrase it."

"All right then, I would ask that no harm comes to

Hugh Maguire."

"Request denied," the Divisional Commander replied curtly. "It is not our intention to harm anyone but if the situation calls for force, then force will be applied evenly. We won't have time to protect your 'source', only our officers."
McAuley shifted uncomfortably in his chair, not daring to look at McCormick whose eyes he felt taunting him.

"I feel I must point out," McAuley blustered, "that assets like Maguire are essential to our work."

"I was under the impression that 'our work' was exactly that," the Divisional Commander replied evenly. "Is 'our work' not effective policing, protecting the innocent and saving lives? Maguire may be essential to you but he's expendable in the wider scheme of things. Detective Sergeant McCormick. From your experience and your knowledge of this particular case, is there anything you would like to add?"

McCormick sat at attention. "Well yes sir. I think you are doing everything correctly and I agree with your position regarding this Maguire. His own so-called comrades have condemned him out of their own mouths by confirming his guilt in the murder of Brendan Flynn, a murder Maguire committed to protect himself and a murder that was never solved or, from what I can gather, was ever really investigated. When did we allow terrorists to literally get off with murder?"

"What are you trying to say?" McAuley bellowed. "Do you honestly believe I gave Maguire free rein to do as he pleased? I will not be defamed like this by anyone, never mind an outsider!"

"Calm down, Jim!" the Divisional Commander snapped. "No one is accusing you of anything! However, accusations of this kind are common in the murky world of informers. That can be rectified by arresting McDermott and whoever comes to collect him in the morning. If that turns out to be Maguire, he will be arrested and imprisoned with his passenger. If either of them pose a risk to my officers, that risk will be eliminated. Now let's look at how we will do this."

-----------------------------------------------------------------

Bryce sat alone in his living room considering the situation. He cursed Maguire and his desperate never ending quest to impress the Belfast boys. Undoubtedly it was that running after them that brought them down here in the first place. He rubbed his face as if that might make all his troubles disappear or give him an answer to his problems. Would there be no end to that McDermott and the trouble that followed him around the country? And Maguire? Bryce shuddered as he thought about his suspicions of that 'Super Republican'. He felt he could tenuously connect Maguire to several arms finds, having spoken to younger volunteers off the record; young men who admitted that they may have mentioned something about the locations of arms to others and Maguire's name came up every time. Bryce sat contemplating his next move for a few hours before reaching a decision.

---

The Divisional Commander also contemplated his situation and the dilemmas that seemed to engulf him. McDermott was tucked away in a supposed safe house oblivious to the fact that the police were monitoring his every word and move. Maguire was a paid informer, something the Divisional Commander despised as much as McCormick. McAuley was running Maguire and keen to protect his source. McCormick seemed content to stay out the way and allow the local police to get on with things. McAuley had been silenced at the meeting but could he be trusted? Would he tip off his source? Though unthinkable, this was entirely possible in the murky world of agents and informers where the officer running the agent could very easily adopt a strange loyalty to his source. After an hour of deliberations, the Divisional Commander knew what he had to do and began to make his preparations.

The officer commanding the E4A unit surrounding the disused cottage checked his watch. It had been a long and uncomfortable few hours as he waited in the constant rain for some movement. The smell of burning logs and peat had been filling his nostrils for ages and he cursed silently as he imagined the Provo in the cottage lying in front of a blazing fire sound asleep whilst he became saturated with the deluge from the heavens. All of his men were in strategic positions around the cottage and they were all well briefed on what to do when the time came. He glanced at his watch again. Would this night ever end? he thought morosely.

---

Jim McAuley sipped a hot whiskey and thought about Hugh Maguire. He owed the ill-tempered Republican a lot and he knew it. Those arms finds, the arrest of Joey Maguire and his colleagues all were all credited to him. Yes, he hated Maguire in one way but Maguire had helped his career in Special Branch. He then thought about the Divisional Commander and frowned. A pompous know-it-all who's ideas about policing came from another era. And McCormick! He had never liked that by-the-book plod with his air of superiority and his smart mouth. He also resented the fact that the DC seemed to share McCormick's contempt for Special Branch and the use of informers. They liked sleuthing and rummaging through rubbish bins looking for clues like cartoon characters. McAuley laughed as he imagined them dressed in Macintoshes with huge magnifying glasses on the trail of a missing cat. Plods! Then he thought about his age, nearness to retirement and his pension. Maybe Maguire was expendable after all ……

---

At the same time, Hugh Maguire was sipping a lukewarm cup of coffee, unable to sleep. His gut instinct told him to send Declan McAleer to pick up McDermott a few hours from then. He would call big McAuley and let him know the time of the pick-up and the peelers would have a wanted IRA man *and* a useless novice to boot. When he had suggested McAleer to Bryce, he saw how the O/C flinched with discomfort and then agreed reluctantly to make contact with his prize pupil. Maguire sniggered as he thought of that skinny good-for-nothing lying face down in the mud with cops all around him. It would rule him out from being the informer, true, but there were others he could point to, including Bryce himself. Contented, he made a brief call to McAuley who was non-committal as always, before going to bed and into a deep sleep.

---

Declan McAleer was surprised when Jim Bryce called at his home at dawn. With no small degree of trepidation, he answered the door and let his O/C into the heat of the house.

"I had a visit last night from Maguire. He will probably either phone you or call here looking for you to do something for him. Now listen carefully. Things are changing and I need you alive and well and out of jail so I want you to make sure you aren't here when Maguire calls either way. Have you access to a car or any type of vehicle?"

"Aye I can borrow my ma's car," McAleer replied cautiously. "But what about Maguire? He will be raging if he comes looking for me and I am not here."

"Let me worry about him, " Bryce replied. "He's a loose cannon and you're better having nothing to do with him. Now go and get dressed and take yourself off somewhere well out of the road, like up to Derry or somewhere. Spend the day there and come home this evening. I was never here and we never had this conversation. OK?"

Declan nodded and Bryce left him to get dressed and be on his way. The C/C got into his car and drove to a small house near the hamlet of Drumagarner and aroused the young occupant from his sleep. He gave the sleepy twenty-something directions to the empty cottage (which was a simple task considering it was only a couple of miles away) instructing him to collect the man there and take him to an address in Dungiven. On the way home, Bryce salved his conscience by arguing with himself that if he was wrong, the young man and McDermott would be out of his area in two hours' time and, if he was right, they would both be in prison by lunchtime. That would be an interesting turn of events given that the driver he had just visited was Hugh Maguire's nephew, Damien. If, as Bryce suspected, Hugh was working for the security forces, he will have put his own nephew in prison as well as the lad's father. If it happens that way, Bryce mused, then Internal Security would be brought in and Hugh would be answering questions in South Armagh with a bag over his head. Either way, this will bring the whole sorry mess to a conclusion.

---

It was a little before daybreak when Damien Maguire arrived at the cottage. A thin wisp of smoke rose from the ancient chimney and blew in Damien's direction as he alighted from the car. That was the only evidence that someone was in the house. Being inexperienced and eager to be of service to the movement, Damien quickly entered the squat dwelling by the back door. He called out softly in case he spooked whoever was inside. Bryce had given him no information whatsoever on the temporary occupant of the house, just where he was to take him. A thrill of excitement ran through Damien's whole body as he moved cautiously into the living room from the small kitchen.

"Who is that?" demanded a voice from the darkness of the smoky, dingy room.

"I am here to take you to your next stop," Damien half-whispered, unsure of what to say or do.

"Who sent you?" the voice asked.

"The local Commanding Officer. He didn't tell me your name so I won't be telling you his!"

Damien then heard a fumbling from the back of the room and then saw an old Tilly lamp starting to glow. As it brightened, he saw the face of a stranger who looked almost as worried and frightened as himself. McDermott nodded in appreciation of the young man's appreciation for security.

"Give me two minutes to put some bits and pieces in a hold-all and we'll be on our way."

Damien thought about going out to the car and getting it started in preparation for the journey but then decided he would wait the two minutes the stranger requested. Looking around the dark, stinking room, Damien made a mental note to make his fight for Ireland's freedom happen far from rat infested hovels like this. The stranger then extinguished the oil lamp and they stepped outside. Damien paused for a moment to light a cigarette, offering the stranger one. The stranger declined the offer with a wave of his hand and suddenly the peace of the early morning was shattered by a booming voice.

"This is the police! Put your hands on your head and get down on your knees. Now!"

Damien dropped his cigarette in shock and terror. He could see no one but whoever was out there could see him. He stood frozen to the spot like a rabbit caught in headlights. McDermott had a little more experience but the shock affected him in a different way. Instead of placing his hands on his head as ordered, he lifted one of his hold-alls in to his chest in a futile but instinctive bid to protect himself. It was then the shooting started. Damien at first felt no pain as the bullets slammed into his torso, hitting him in the chest and spinning him around with the force of it. More rounds hit him in the back but he never knew because before he hit the ground, Damien Maguire was dead.

The first round fired at McDermott caught him in the thigh, followed by more rounds that embedded themselves in the hold-all. Desperately McDermott leapt to the side, the pain excruciating, and rolled into a hedge. Abandoning the hold-all, he got up painfully and stumbled towards the front of the house, unable to see where he was going. After a few steps he tripped over the remains of a rotting fence and fell headlong into the unruly hedge growing alongside the house. Behind him he heard shouting and footsteps crunching across the stones so he got up as quickly as possible and ran blindly, not knowing where he was going.

"Stop right now and put your hands on your head!" a voice commanded in front of him.

McDermott didn't have time to think. He took another two steps and the E4A officer opened fire, cutting McDermott down. Lifelessly he fell heavily on his back, his career as a member of the IRA over forever.

In the police station, the Divisional Commander sat listening in the Ops Room waiting to hear from the E4A team surrounding the old cottage. Smith sat alongside him along with McAuley and McCormick paced up and down the cramped room getting more and more agitated as each minute passed.

Suddenly the tense silence was broken by the cracking sound of a radio. The Divisional Commander grabbed a set of headphones and spoke to the voice on the other end. It was a brief conversation and when it was over, he turned to the others.

"Well gentlemen, it looks like the job has been done bringing an end to this whole sorry episode. That report confirmed that an unknown person arrived at the cottage and after going inside for a few minutes, came out with McDermott. They were ordered to stop and place their hands on their heads but they foolishly refused. The officers on the ground had no choice but open fire. Both suspects died at the scene."

The others maintained silence for a few moments before McAuley spoke.

"We know McDermott was one of the suspects but have we any idea who the other one is? I am asking because Hugh Maguire called me in the early hours to tip me off that McDermott was at the cottage and would be collected this morning. I can't imagine the other person is Maguire as he would hardly set himself up. He's stupid but not *that* stupid."

Smith answered, "We have no intelligence as to the identity of the second man although I can confirm that McDermott was one of the deceased."

A discussion then commenced as to how to handle the aftermath of the incident. After half an hour of planning and suggestions, the meeting was interrupted by a uniformed constable who discreetly passed a folded note to the Divisional Commander who read the contents impassively as the others waited with silent anticipation. As if responding to their questioning looks, the Divisional Commander cleared his throat and looked directly at McAuley before speaking.
"It would seem that there is a very good chance that your friend Maguire is indeed as stupid as he looks if this report is correct. After a cursory search of the car at the scene, there is evidence that suggests that the identity of the second man is one "*HD Maguire*" and although that's not necessary your *Hugh* Maguire, it may very well be."

McAuley stared back, his eyes bulging and then scanned the room as if looking reassurance that this couldn't be true. Everyone seemed unable to hold his glare and McAuley sank back in his seat, speechless with shock. None of it made sense.

The meeting was quickly adjourned with the

Divisional Commander warning everyone that there was a press blackout and that the press office would inform the public of the incident, adding that the identities of both men had not been officially confirmed.

---

McAuley left the station immediately after the meeting ended, speaking to no one on his way out. He drove for about half a mile and then parked the car near a telephone box. Breathless with fear and panic, he dialled Maguire's number. After a few rings, it was answered.

"Are you OK?" McAuley demanded.

"Aye of course I am!" Maguire snapped. "Just sitting here waiting word on what went down, if anything."

"Oh a lot has gone down!" McAuley assured him. "Including you, we thought."

"What are you going on about, McAuley?"

"Well, I was in the station when the report came through. Looks like E4a took McDermott out and whoever called to collect him too. Both men confirmed dead though the identities haven't officially been released to us."

Maguire's eyes lit up with anticipation. McDermott is dead and McAleer too! Bryson is finished, he thought smiling. A hassle eliminated and a cowardly runt into the bargain and all under Bryson's watch. But what did McAuley mean when he said 'Including you'?

"What did you mean by that at the start of the conversation?" Maguire asked, suddenly uneasy.

"When we were discussing what had happened, a plod came in with a note and passed it to the Boss. He read it and then said McDermott was one of the two shot dead and the other was H Maguire. Well, naturally I thought ....."

"He said that? He said H Maguire? What age?"

"I don't know but that's what he said. HD Maguire. It must have been some form of identification in his car."

The line went dead and McAuley looked at the receiver and then shrugged his shoulders, replacing it and deciding to go home for a few hours. It had been a long night and he was suddenly very tired.

Maguire looked wide eyed around the empty room. It couldn't be! It couldn't be his nephew, Damien! Hugh Damien Maguire! Aw please no! What about McAleer? Bryson was meant to send McAleer! There's definitely something sly about that boy! And Justine! She will be heartbroken; her man in jail and now her son lying dead in a mortuary slab! Joey will go insane, locked up in a cell trying to deal with the death of his son! In a fit of temper and despair,

Maguire viciously kicked over the ancient coffee table, sending a mug crashing against the wall and scattering papers and magazines like confetti all over the floor.

After his rage had slightly abated, he tried to think about what to do next. One thing he was certain about; he would hang the blame for this on Declan McAleer. He never liked McAleer with his cowardly, snivelling ways and he could never understand why Bryson protected him. Yes, McAleer was quite well-read and knew all about the history of Republicanism but he *wasn't* one. He was just a wannabe, a cheerleader who liked to be seen with real Republicans without becoming one in any real sense. Well, Maguire resolved, if he didn't like the idea of firing a gun at someone, he won't like one being fired into him! Without further ado, Maguire grabbed his car keys from the grubby mat and charged out of his house to see Bryce.

Jim Bryce stood looking blankly out of his living room window sipping a mug of hot coffee. He had heard on the radio that two suspected terrorists had been shot dead but their names hadn't been released. Bryce had turned off the radio; he didn't need to hear any more and he already knew the names of the dead.

Sean McDermott, former darling of the Belfast Brigade and Damien Maguire, young and naïve who lived in awe of his irrational uncle Hugh. Although

Bryce didn't know it was going to end this way, he had his suspicions. Hugh Maguire had been too adamant that young McAleer would have to be on the job. Bryce had been in the IRA long enough to develop a sixth sense for these things. Maguire had been involved in too many things that had gone wrong and tragically wrong at that. There was the arrest of his brother followed by Maguire's insistence that young Flynn had set him up. Bryce never believed that Flynn had played any part in the arrest of Joey Maguire and he had been furious when the young man wound up dead. No court martial, no proper enquiries, nothing. It had been Maguire shifting the blame from himself to a young, innocent volunteer to cover his tracks and protect himself. Brendan Flynn, a young idealistic man who wanted to fight for Ireland, beaten and drowned by the real informer. That was how Bryce read it now though even back then he had had his doubts. And then there was the massacre at McCormick's house. Maguire had been in the area and managed to evade all of the roadblocks the whole way from Crumlin to Kilrea. And now this. Bryce sighed deeply as his eye caught sight of Maguire's car pulling up outside his house. Setting his mug down by the window, he braced himself for what was to come. This is why some are leaders and others need led, he thought glumly.

"What exactly happened this morning?" Maguire barked as he entered the house.

"It all went wrong, Hugh," Bryce replied quietly.

"*It all went wrong?*" Maguire repeated incredulously, glaring at the Commanding Officer. "Is that it? Is that all you have to say? My nephew is lying dead on a slab!"

"I know, Hugh, and I can hardly take it in. He had plenty of promise and McDermott's skills will be hard to replace. It was clearly a set-up like the others. I mean, like the attempt on McCormick."

Maguire studied Bryce carefully. Now was his chance.

"Well, that's it! There's a tout and I have a fair idea who it is, too. Declan McAleer! I know you have a soft spot for him, Jim, but it *has* to be him. He never gets involved in the thick of things, never dirties his hands, yet he's always sneaking about wanting to know everything, following you about like a lap dog. Now why would he want to know everything yet take care not to *do* anything? It's a text book case, Jim!"

"Much as I hate to admit it but you're right, Hugh. I have harboured some suspicions about Declan for some time now."

Encouraged by Bryce's verbal thoughts, Maguire continued, his excitement rising.

"Was he not meant to be on the job this morning? Did we not agree that he would pick McDermott up and take him out of there?"

Bryce nodded, staring Maguire in the eye. "Aye, I called with him yesterday and asked him to collect McDermott but he made up some excuse that he had somewhere to go and wouldn't be about all day. I wondered about that but then thought it was just him being his usual cagey self but now, with all that's happened ....."

"So he *knew* McDermott was getting picked up this morning! What more proof do you need, Jim? It has been McAleer the whole time!"

As Bryce sat heavily on one of the two armchairs in the room, Maguire decided to destroy his nemesis once and for all.

"And what about all the wee arms finds, Jim? A gun here, a few rounds there. Never enough to attract too much attention yet always enough to damage the movement. And then there's the question of the hit on McCormick's house. How do you know McAleer knew nothing about that? Him and House Malone were very close, Jim. Who's to say House didn't confide in him and that wee scumbag rang his handler first chance he got? We have to bring him in, Jim! Want me to go get him?"

Jim sighed. "No, it's OK Hugh. He's my problem so I will go and get him. Anyway, he's already scared of you so if you arrive at his house he might take off or cause a scene and we don't want that with his parents and all in the house. He told me he's away for most of the day so I will leave it until evening but I want you here, Hugh. I admit I have a liking for him and it won't be easy sending him to what will undoubtedly be his death."

"What do you mean *sending* him? Sending him where? This is a local issue, Jim. We should be dealing with this ourselves!"

"Just a figure of speech, Hugh. Call back here at 8pm and I will have him here. Maybe you should go and see Justine and giver her some support. And, if you have time, get on to the solicitor and tell him to make an application to get Joey compassionate leave from the Blocks. He should be with his wife so they can mourn their son together."

Maguire nodded and left without another word and Bryce pulled on his coat before setting off to Belfast. This is a job for Internal Security and not something that can be discussed over a phone. As he drove off, he felt a slight pang of guilt-or was it regret- but quickly shook it off and continued on his journey.

## Chapter 12

### *The Web Untangles*

"Well, Jim, it looks like the threat has abated," Smith told his old friend as they relaxed over two whiskey and water.

"How can you be so sure?" McCormick asked, unconvinced.

"The threat against you emanated from your identification of Sean McDermott. The rule of thumb appears to have been that you had to go to protect him. With you dead, McDermott would be safe to carry on his bomb making activities so it was imperative that they eliminated you as soon as possible. My sources tell me that our friend McDermott became something of a hot potato up here and there wasn't a great deal of enthusiasm amongst local Republicans when it came to keeping him safe. Although he hailed from North Antrim, it seems he had little or nothing to do with the local men and they regarded him as Belfast's problem, not theirs. Anyway, with him dead, the locals can breathe easy again and there is no longer any need to take you out."

McCormick nodded thoughtfully. "And after the reception they got at my house the other night, they will be in no hurry to come for me again, I suppose."

"Exactly! I suppose you will be heading back to Belfast soon?"

"Are you asking me or telling me, Smithy?" McCormick said, brightening at the thought of being a thorn in the side of local police. "Is it you who's asking or did the D.C suggest you ask it?"

Smith smiled and shook his head. "Just a routine enquiry, Jim. No need to go on the offensive every time someone says something."

McCormick glanced sceptically at his friend. "I suppose I will head back shortly. Maybe tomorrow or I might just wait until after the funeral. Bryson and Greer will have been lost without me and knowing McCrum, he has been throwing tenners at that dipstick McNamee and he will expect the same from me but, as you know, I .."

"Never pay touts! I know, Jim, you have oft repeated that to me. Do you mind if I make a suggestion, though, maybe offer some advice? Although you don't want to admit it, things are changing. I am not privy to the details but even though it doesn't look like it at times, Republicans are edging towards a ceasefire. I have heard it at meetings, on the ground and it would seem that even local IRA members accept the fact that this phase of violence is drawing to a close. Sinn Fein is being feted and lauded throughout the country and further afield. My reading of Irish history is that the end is nigh, as it were. You have to admit that although the McDermott's of this world have been keeping the pot boiling, IRA violence is already on the decline. Historically, this is the modus operandi that results in a ceasefire. As things change, we will have to change too, Jim. Instead of paramilitary violence we will be tackling ordinary crime. Now, Greer and Bryson are better placed to know what's going on than me or you but that is likely why they try to place a restraining arm on you. Do you understand what I'm saying?"

McCormick remained silent for a few minutes, staring at the bright flames licking the seasoned logs on the open fire. Smith wondered if he had even heard what had been said for his benefit. Finally McCormick looked at Smith and nodded ruefully.
"I know, Smithy. I have seen it and heard it all lately and even though I don't cosy up to politicians, it's pretty obvious that there's something in the air. I will never be a lap dog to Greer and Bryson and their kind. They have just accepted it and will do whatever the politicians tell them to do. But that's not me! I realise I will have to go along with it but I don't have to like it and I don't have to make things pleasant for Greer and Bryson. Maybe I should look at another career, Smithy. It could be that I have outgrown the police."

Smith laughed scornfully. "You were born for the police, Jim. You couldn't live without it!"

-------------------------------------------------------------------

Hugh Maguire crumpled a little when he came face to face with his sister-in-law. Justine was distraught with grief over the death of her eldest son and her face was etched in misery and bewilderment. The moment she saw Hugh, she ran to him and embraced him, hugging his body tightly to hers and sobbing noisily into his chest. Maguire didn't know how to handle this heartbreaking outpouring of grief and simply responded by lightly rubbing her upper arms. He was further stung by the grief torn looks of older family members who had gathered and a disapproving glare from the local priest who knew Maguire's past.

After comforting Justine as best he could in his usual awkward fashion, Maguire found a seat tucked into the corner of the cramped living room. He felt a tightening in his chest as he observed the bewildered family and friend of Joey and Justine Maguire. He wanted desperately to leave this house of pain, pain he had caused not once, but twice. Then he realised that the feelings that were encompassing him were driven by something he had never experienced before; *guilt.* Yes he had persuaded everyone that Flynn had been responsible for Joey's imprisonment and he had even gotten off with murdering the hapless Flynn but here, today, the realisation of all the hurt he had caused hit him like a sledgehammer. His thoughts then turned to McAleer, the perfect scapegoat. He wanted to be the one to interrogate him but maybe Bryce was right to send him away for questioning. The boys in the Internal Security unit will turn the screws on McAleer and by the time they are finished with him, he will admit to anything. He allowed himself a half smile as he thought about that spineless lackey crying for his mother and admitting to the arms and munitions finds, the deaths of the boys at McCormick's house and the recent deaths of McDermott and young Damien. And then he was uncomfortably aware of someone staring at him, eyes boring deep inside him. He turned and looked towards the doorway and there was Dab Brennan, the local village idiot, looking at him with what seemed like a mixture of hatred and resentment. Maguire scowled back but Dab kept his penetrating stare fixed on him. It was time to go, Maguire decided. He offered to go and see the solicitor to arrange Joey's compassionate leave from the Maze prison. Justine thanked him over and over which only added to Maguire's discomfort so he left as quickly as possible.

At tea time, on his return from Belfast, Jim Bryce called on the grieving family. Justine seemed glad to see him and agreed to his request that the young lad should be given a Republican funeral with the tricolour over the coffin along with a beret and gloves with a piper leading the cortège. Bryce assured Justine that he would take care of all of the arrangements and that young Damien would get the send-off he deserved. After staying a few minutes more to speak to other mourners, Bryce left to return home to await his guests for the evening.

At seven o'clock in the evening, Hugh Maguire pulled up outside Him Bryce's modest home. Checking around the house as was his custom, he noticed Bryce's car and another one in front of it partially hidden from view. Before entering the house, he examined the strange car closer and noted that it bore registration plates from the Republic of Ireland. A thrill of excitement surged through his body as he realised that they were already here; Internal Security AKA the Nutting Squad. As he knocked the heavy front door, Maguire smiled. Maybe if McAleer is deemed responsible for all of the recent mishaps and mayhem, he will feel better. And Bryce! He will look so stupid when it turns out that his prize pupil is found to be responsible for five deaths and everything else to boot. Surely this will be the end of Bryce, thereby clearing the way for him to take over as Commanding Officer.

"Hi Hugh!" Bryce said in greeting before following his visitor into the living room, "how's it going?
I called in with Justine earlier and they all seemed to be bearing up OK. Did you see the solicitor about getting Joey out for the funeral?"

Maguire threw himself into an armchair. "Aye they'll be all right. I saw the solicitor surely and they can't see a problem getting Joey out. I will go up and pick him up as soon as I get the word. Where's McAleer?"

"Take it easy, Hugh," Bryce cautioned, "all in good time. There are a few things we need to chat about before we take the next step. Hold on there where you're at so the others can join us and give us their opinions."

Bruce then opened the door leading to his kitchen and made way for three strangers who came in silently, one of them taking position at the door leading to the hallway, one remaining at the door he had just entered and the third joining Bryce of the sofa. Maguire felt a little uneasy as it was a small room and the presence of another three men seemed to fill the void.

"Hugh, there are a few things bothering me so I spent the best part of the day in the city speaking to one of these men here. He then sent for his two friends and they came down here to see if they can find answers to the questions that have evaded me until now."

"Questions about McAleer, you mean?" Maguire asked hopefully.

"No, Hugh, questions about you. That time your Joey was caught, it seems to me that you were privy to all of the information about that hit. The only thing you didn't know was that Joey stepped in at the last minute. I believe that you set them boys up and you put your own brother in jail. Then, to cover it up, you picked a clean young Republican, Brendan Flynn, a young man with plenty of ability, and set him up to take the blame for what *you did."*

Maguire sat forward in his chair and laughed harshly.

"What are you on about, Bryce? Are you listening to yourself? You've spent far too long out of the action! That is about as mad a tale as I have ever heard!"

Bryce continued as if Maguire hadn't spoken. "You couldn't risk having Flynn questioned as it would have proved his innocence so you proclaimed him guilty, killed him without permission and tossed his body into the Bann. At the time we were angry that you done that but, at the same time, we understood that you were insane with anger over Joey's imprisonment so we let it go. We were actually convinced for a while that you were right about Flynn and our faith in your judgement was such that we thought you wouldn't have acted in such an extreme way unless you had proof. It was a failing in my part that we didn't investigate further and I admit that but the truth is that you were the one who put Joey in jail and you set up Flynn as the perpetrator, sending a good young man to his death to save yourself. Then there were all the wee arms finds, a few rounds here, the odd gun there. Again that was you."

Maguire glared at his accuser before looking at the other men in the room. "He hates me! This is a personal vendetta! He is no Commander! Do you boys see what I have had to put up with all this time?"

The words were brave but Maguire was afraid and his voice betrayed him.

"And then there was McDermott. You arranged for him to be brought here and agreed that we would hide him and take out the cop in Crumlin. It was almost a replica of the night Joey was caught, wasn't it? You sowed the seeds of doubt about young McAleer, hinting and then insisting that he was an informer to cover up your part in the finds and the deaths of the young men who were cut to bits at McCormick's house that night before you set up who you believed was McAleer. Of course, you got it wrong again and another member of your family suffered for your treachery. You really are a piece of work, Maguire. I couldn't think why you did all this until I finally worked it all out. It was me. You couldn't accept that the Brigade Staff made me Commanding Officer instead of you. You done all this to undermine me and you know what all of this proves? That the Brigade Staff were right all along. You weren't fit for the job and you never would be. Well, we are at the end of the road now, Hugh. You will accompany these men to South Armagh right now. I don't expect to see or hear from you again."

Suddenly Maguire lunged at Bryce from his sitting position, his arms outstretched but before he could make contact with his intended victim, the man standing at the door nearest him grabbed him, pinning him firmly to his seat. The man beside Bryce got up and pointed a handgun at Maguire as the third man pulled cable ties from his jacket pocket. In a few minutes, Hugh Maguire was standing with his hands behind his back bound tightly with the cable ties and makeshift cuffs around his ankles, allowing only the minimum of movement. Bryce looked on impassively as he was pushed out of the back door of his house to the car with the Southern registration. The man with the gun nodded at Bryce and left wordlessly, slamming the back door behind him. Bryce watched from his window as the car drove off and then placed a call to Declan McAleer, inviting him round for a chat.

McAleer was shocked to hear everything that had transpired in the past twenty-four hours. As instructed, he had taken off early in the morning and spent the day with his cousins in their home in Dungiven. He had heard about the double killing on the radio and was shocked to learn that Damien Maguire was one of the victims. Declan knew Damien to see and wasn't even aware he was in the IRA.

"Declan, young Damien hero worshipped his uncle Hugh and wanted to be a man like him. In fact, he was already showing signs of being exactly like his uncle. He would likely have turned out as unmanageable and unpredictable."

"But why did Hugh Maguire hate me so much?" Declan asked genuinely interested to know the reason.

"Hugh hated life, the world and everyone else in it but most of all he hated himself. He was just one of life's mysteries who would have had a blood lust no matter where he had been born. He hated you because you weren't like him. He resented your knowledge, intelligence and, above all, your humanity. This thing is coming to an end and it will be the likes of you who will take the movement forward politically. Hugh wanted nothing to do with that and young Damien would have taken his lead from his uncle. He hated me too because I can see what's happening and I agree with it. All the deaths and miseries of the last two decades and for what? Where is our United Ireland? The Brits love political settlements and they won't care how that pans out. The Unionists can't see that in their blind loyalty to the Crown but mark my words, if the majority goes for a United Ireland, the Brits will grant it. From now until then they will likely create the circumstances that will make that achievable and that's where you come in. You are the future, Declan, and you will have my full support."

"But what about Maguire?"

"Don't worry about him," Bryce said absently. "He will be questioned and sentenced according to our rules. What happens next will also be done according to our rules. It will be right and proper." As he said these words, Bryce shuddered as he thought about the techniques that would be used by Internal Security to illicit the information they sought. Hugh will get all the violence he wants, mused Bryce grimly.

---

"Welcome home, Jim!" John McCrum exclaimed as McCormick strode into the police station and sat down heavily on his worn swivel chair. "Did you have a nice time away?"

McCormick smiled. McCrum was learning the tools of the trade; quips and sarcasm. He will do all right.

"Aye it was quite refreshing, John. I caught up with a few friends from the old days and a few from the old days almost caught up with me! How's things with you? Have you been good to my adopted son, Joe McNamee?"

"We have an understanding. He's all yours now and I do think you should reward him in some way as he did try to save your life, though who knows why?"

McCormick responded with a sarcastic smile that looked more like a grimace. "How's my old mucker Felix?"

"Oh haven't you heard? He has been kicked upstairs to make Greer's lunches and so on. The new boss is more like us though we have officially been told to adopt a softly softly approach when dealing with the Provos. Seems that Sinn Fein are taking over so we have to adapt to the idea of the tail wagging the dog."

"Well, well! This is all very refreshing news, John! Maybe the Provos finally got the message! There's no killing McCormick!

## Epilogue

Jim McCormick continued to serve in the RUC until his retirement from the force. After the 1994 ceasefire he was involved in smashing a group of dissenting Republicans in Belfast.

John McCrum remained good friends with McCormick and also remained in the RUC until he took a job in a Consultancy firm after McCormick retired.

Joe McNamee remained on the fringes of the Republican movement but drifted away after the 1994 ceasefire. His former comrades never discovered he had been an informer for years.

Jim Bryce remained as the Commanding Officer of the IRA in his area until 1997 when he suffered a diabetic stroke. He was in a coma for five weeks before dying in the presence of close family members.

Daniel "Dab" Brennan continued to wander the roads of Swatragh and Kilrea until his mother died after which he became a resident in a care home where he kept himself busy by tending the gardens and telling wild stories to the other residents including one where a mysterious person called Cormac was being hunted for death by bad boys.

Justine Maguire was reunited with her husband Joey after his release from the Maze prison and, a few months later, they moved to Donegal where Joey found work with a haulage firm.

Declan McAleer eventually became a Sinn Fein councillor with unswerving loyalty to the Belfast leadership.

Hugh Maguire was never seen again after the night he was led from Jim Bryce's home. It was believed that he was shot dead after admitting his role as an informer and, to spare his family embarrassment (given their Republican background), he was secretly buried somewhere along the border.

Printed in Great Britain
by Amazon